Pit Bulls vs. Aliens

NEAL WOOTEN

ISBN 978-1-61225-301-5

Published by Mirror Publishing
Milwaukee, WI 53214
www.pagesofwonder.com

Printed in the USA

Acknowledgments

A special thanks to all the friends and family who supported the book, as well as these awesome Facebook pages listed below.

Munster:
https://www.facebook.com/MunstersFancyPants

Josh and his critters:
https://www.facebook.com/pages/Josh-and-his-critters/1506300642923754

The Positive Pit Bull:
https://www.facebook.com/pages/The-Positive-Pit-Bull/282575600129

Wallace the Pit Bull:
https://www.facebook.com/WallaceThePitBull

The Truth About Pit Bulls:
https://www.facebook.com/pages/The-Truth-About-Pit-Bulls/231633676863468

Brad's Pit:
https://www.facebook.com/pages/Brads-Pit/332755236863042

Patch O'Pits Therapy Dogs:
https://www.facebook.com/PatchOPitsTherapyDogs

Bodacious the Super Hero Pit Bull Therapy Dog:
https://www.facebook.com/BodaciousTheSuperHeroPitBullTherapy-Dog

Auggie & Company:
https://www.facebook.com/RunAuggieRun

For Real Pit Bull Lovers:
https://www.facebook.com/ForRealPitBullLovers

Acknowledgments (cont.)

Sadie the Pibble Mix:
https://www.facebook.com/SadieThePibbleMix

Pullin 4 Bullies:
https://www.facebook.com/Pullin4Bullies

Pibble – Pawsitively Inspiring Bully Breed Lovers Everywhere:
https://www.facebook.com/PIBBLE2

Cora the Wobbly Pittie Girl:
https://www.facebook.com/CoraTheWobblyPittieGirl

Life with Lilah:
https://www.facebook.com/LifeWithLilah

The Walking Dead Fan Club:
https://www.facebook.com/WalkingDead4

Table of Contents

Acknowledgments..3

Chapter One..7

Chapter Two..15

Chapter Three..23

Chapter Four..31

Chapter Five..39

Chapter Six..47

Chapter Seven..55

Chapter Eight..63

Chapter Nine..71

Chapter Ten..79

Chapter Eleven..88

Chapter Twelve..97

Chapter Thirteen..105

Chapter Fourteen..114

Chapter Fifteen..122

Chapter Sixteen..130

Chapter Seventeen..138

Chapter Eighteen..147

Chapter Nineteen..155

Chapter Twenty..164

Chapter Twenty-One..171

Neal Wooten

1

"It's Hangar 51."

"Beg pardon?"

Thomas Freeman tugged at the knot on his tie. He had to wear a button extension just to get the collar to fasten around his thick neck, and it was not easy to breathe. "It's not Area 51. The real place where the aliens crash-landed and the alien autopsies were conducted is officially titled Hangar 51."

Burt Smellie, the host of the comedy talk show *Psycho America*, stared across the table at his guest. Coarse black hairs peeked out from the unbuttoned shirt of his three-piece suit. The black hairpiece that perched on his crown did not match the salt-and-pepper strands that grew down the sides and back of his head. His short, heavyset frame almost seemed to balance on his chair. Large gold rings dug into the flesh of his nubby fingers, making them look like sausage links. "Are you sure? I've always heard it called Area 51. I have records going back for a long time using the name Area 51."

Thomas shook his head. "The government installation in Roswell is Hangar 51. Area 51 in Nevada is a decoy used for a tourist attraction. A long time ago, some Hollywood people asked permission to use Hangar 51 in a movie and the government refused. They invented Area 51 for the movie, and it stuck. The media ran with it and now that's where people think the aliens landed."

Mr. Smellie opened his eyes and mouth wide to exaggerate his disbelief. "But the government says that too. Why would they do that?"

"Why wouldn't they? It makes it easier to hide the files. That's

7

just part of the government cover-up," Thomas said.

"Oh right," Mr. Smellie said with a smirk. "Ye old government cover-up."

The audience laughed.

"Tell me, Mr. Freeman, do you really believe that an alien crash-landed way back in 1950 and the government was able to keep everyone from finding out about it?"

Thomas nodded. "I do."

"Of course," Mr. Smellie said. "And all the UFO sightings are real, I suppose."

"No, of course not." Thomas cocked his head to one side. "I mean, someone seeing something might be real, but they're not all alien spacecraft."

"How many are, then?" Mr. Smellie asked. "Ten percent? Fifty percent? Ninety-nine?"

Thomas adjusted his tie again. "Probably only a very small percentage."

"And the rest are what—wackos looking for attention?" Mr. Smellie leaned forward and raised his eyebrows.

Thomas shrugged. "I know your thing is to have people on and make fun of them. I know ratings are far more important than anything else. But there have been over two million documented sightings of strange aircraft. The question is, do you believe they're all fake?"

"I do, I really do," Mr. Smellie said, to the delight of the people in the studio watching the live broadcast. He certainly knew how to work a crowd. "There have been just as many Bigfoot sightings. Do you believe in Bigfoot?"

"No."

"Ah," Mr. Smellie said. "So you believe they're all wackos too?"

This guy is good, Thomas thought. "I don't know. Just because I don't believe in Bigfoot doesn't mean it doesn't exist."

There were a few scattered claps from the audience.

"Fair enough, Mr. Freeman," Mr. Smellie said. "But tell me, why do you think these aliens spying on us have never made contact?"

"I don't know. I suspect they will when they're ready."

"Okay, good answer," Mr. Smellie said. The crowd was silent, and he apparently didn't like that. When they're silent, it means they're actually listening to the guest, and that was not something Burt Smellie tolerated. "We're going to break away for our sponsors, ladies and gentlemen. Don't go away; we'll be right back."

The stage was suddenly illuminated as a woman came out to touch up Mr. Smellie's makeup.

Thomas tried to adjust his suit. Normally all he ever wore were shorts, T-shirts, or sweats with flip-flops or sandals. He was six feet five and very muscular with a thin waist. He spent six years in the Marines and still put in ten hours a week at the gym lifting heavy weights. This suit, the one he reserved for weddings and funerals, was not him, but he wanted to look good for television. Even his long dark-brown hair was in a ponytail, and his beard and mustache were neat and trimmed. Of course he realized that "looking good" might not be possible for this show. He knew what the show, not to mention the host, was all about, but an author never turns down a chance for publicity, no matter what form it might come in.

He looked around at the cheap set with its flimsy cardboard backdrop. The stage lights were actually draped over metal rafters by their cords. The viewers' seats were simple folding chairs on a scuffed tile floor. As Thomas looked out over the members of the audience, he suspected they were mostly friends, family, or staff members of Mr. Smellie.

And there was a familiar smell in the room that tickled his olfactory senses. It was the combination of toxic fumes mixed with burned ozone, like an electrical fire. Thomas searched the floor where all the bundles of twisted cables and cords ran in all directions, looking for a telltale sign of white plumes of smoke, but saw nothing. Suddenly the smell hit him harder, and he looked up to see the makeup girl fanning Mr. Smellie with a cardboard handheld fan. That's when he realized the smell was coming from his gracious host, no doubt a combination of body odor and cheap cologne. "Smellie" was certainly a good name for him.

"You're doing well," Mr. Smellie said. "It's all in fun; give and take."

Thomas looked up to see Mr. Smellie going through his notes. "Are you talking to me?"

"Of course," Mr. Smellie answered without looking up. It appeared that Thomas's answers were not crazy enough for him to make jokes about. He needed to beef it up. That's why he was skimming through the notes.

The lights dimmed and the show resumed.

"And we're back. Our guest today is alien enthusiast, alien believer, alien nutcase Thomas Freeman. Thanks again for joining us. I want to shift gears for a moment. Let's talk about cow mutilations."

Thomas sat quietly.

"Is that okay with you, Mr. Freeman?"

Thomas nodded. "Sure."

Mr. Smellie smiled as if he had just gotten a big game animal to take the bait. "Now I've talked to a lot of crazy alien-conspiracy theorists in my day, and while their delusions come in all shapes and sizes, they all have this one little tidbit in common: cow mutilations are the work of aliens. But looking through your writings, sir, I see that you do not subscribe to that theory. Is that correct?"

"That's correct."

Mr. Smellie turned both hands upright, the palms facing the ceiling. "Anything to add?"

"No."

"Ah come on, Mr. Freeman." Mr. Smellie pointed to his audience. "Our viewers, the ones who were not dropped on their heads as a baby, want to know what wisdom you possess on this. Please elaborate and enlighten us as to what or who has been causing cow mutilations for the last century."

Thomas hesitated. He knew what the reaction would be, but he agreed to come on to the show, so he might as well be honest.

"The government."

The crowd went wild with laughter.

Mr. Smellie made funny faces toward the audience and the cameras to milk the most out of it. "Why, pray tell? Why is Uncle Sam messing with my beef?"

The audience continued to laugh and howl.

Oh heck, Thomas thought, *let's get it over with.* "There have been ninety-one documented cases of cow mutilations in the last one hundred years. All have UFO sightings accompanying the events and always the same MO—the cows are found dead with one jaw removed, the tongue, sex organs, stomach, anal canal, and all the blood removed. And each time it was done with laser surgery. But in 1957, when the first event was investigated, only the government had access to this technique."

"Why, Mr. Freeman?" Mr. Smellie asked. "What does the government need with those things?"

"That's the sixty-four-dollar question, isn't it?" Thomas asked. "But consider this: the government has a huge problem with toxic and nuclear waste with no legitimate way to disburse it. You know what they do with it now?"

Mr. Smellie thought for a second. "Sell it to my mother-in-law for cooking?"

Thomas and the crowd laughed. "Well, maybe, but a lot of it they bury in steel drums somewhere in Idaho, drums that will decay in a couple of hundred years. This is stuff that has a half life of twenty thousand years, which means only in twenty thousand years will it be safe to reintroduce into the environment."

"Okay, I'm following you." Mr. Smellie seemed to forget he was hosting a show making fun of people and started getting into the story. "So what's the connection to the cow murders?"

"Well," Thomas continued, "maybe the government has found a better way. What if they were to spread it out over large rural areas? And if you were to introduce a lethal substance to an area and wanted to evaluate what effects it was having, how would you do it?

"How?" Mr. Smellie asked. "Please don't keep us in suspense."

Thomas continued. "You would want to study an animal that lives directly off the land, and a cow fits the bill. So what parts would you study?"

Mr. Smellie raised his hand like a schoolkid. "I know. I know. Tongue and jaw. Stomach and sex organs. Blood and anal canal. Am I right? Am I right?"

"You're right," Thomas said with a smile. "Let's hear it for him."

The crowd began to applaud and cheer, and right there Mr. Smellie realized he had lost control of them, something a talk show host should never do. This had to be corrected.

"Thank you. Thank you all." Mr. Smellie stood up and blew kisses to the crowd. "Tell him what he's won, Charlie." Mr. Smellie changed the tone of his voice to impersonate his fictional announcer. "You've won a lifetime supply of cow sex organs."

The audience laughed and clapped.

"And what for Mr. Freeman for inventing this ridiculous fallacy?" Again, in his announcer tone, he said, "Mr. Freeman wins a lifetime supply of cow brains, since he clearly chooses not to use his own."

The crowd guffawed, and Thomas nodded at his own gullibility and tugged at his collar to allow more airflow.

After the crowd died down, Mr. Smellie continued. "What's next for you, Thomas Freeman? Any exciting alien adventures on the horizon?"

"Next week a group of us will be picketing the Climatology Department in Washington."

"Well, that sounds like a hoot," Mr. Smellie joked. "So clearly the government is causing global warming as well. Right?"

"I don't believe so," Thomas answered honestly. "But I think they still keep the information from the public."

"That's right," Mr. Smellie said, making a fist and shaking it above his head. "Power to the people. Power to the people. So what is causing global warming? The last three years have been unbearably hot, yet we're told that the greenhouse gas problem was solved a decade ago. You might be on to something here."

"Exactly," Thomas said. "The creation of GHR1101 has done a lot to reduce the amount of greenhouse gases in our atmosphere, so why aren't the temps normalizing?"

"Ah, so it is the government doing it. Just like the killing of our bovines. Is that what you're saying, Mr. Freeman?"

"No," Thomas said. "I think it's aliens."

Mr. Smellie threw his stack of papers in the air as the audience went wild with laughter. "I can't win with this guy. Okay, why would aliens be doing it?"

Thomas could feel the blood building up behind his cheeks, but he fought to contain it. "That's all explained in my new book. Perhaps you've read my books."

"Ah, yes, the books. No, I haven't gotten around to it. We'll get to that later. Let's pretend that my viewers are also normal people who have never read your books. Why would aliens come here?"

"There are several reasons," Thomas began. "Hopefully they would come to share technology. If they're carbon-based life forms like us, they might come for food or water. But since the global temperatures have been increasing at an alarming rate, I believe the aliens are terraforming, which means they will be coming to establish settlements."

"What?" Mr. Smellie shouted. "With humans still here? That would never happen."

"It's already happened."

Mr. Smellie stared at Thomas. "Aliens are already here? Where?"

"Not aliens," Thomas corrected. "When Europeans first came to America, there were already people here. It didn't stop them from setting up colonies."

"Oh my gosh." Mr. Smellie turned to the camera with his mouth wide open and his hands on his cheeks on each side. "That is so true." He looked back to Thomas. "That explains my kid's Thanksgiving painting showing pilgrims, Indians, and aliens."

The crowd erupted again.

"So tell me, Mr. Freeman, if this manic-depressive apocalyptic vision of yours were to come true, if aliens were to ever come to Earth wanting to take over and live here, would we have anything that could stop them?"

Thomas thought for a second. "Nothing I can think of."

Mr. Smellie looked back to the main camera. "And there you have it. That's all the time we have for today. Thanks for tuning in."

"Mr. Smellie?" Thomas said, holding up his book and tapping the cover.

"Oh yes," Mr. Smellie said and held up his copy of the book. "Mr. Freeman's new book is called *Mark My Words: They're Coming*. You can find it in most fringe bookstores in the 'I Can't Believe the Crap They Publish' section. Tune in next week when we talk with a woman who claims her tomatoes speak to her."

And with that the lights came on and the show was over. The audience was dispersed as a woman came over to Thomas to remove the microphone from his lapel.

"That was a great show, Mr. Freeman. You are a natural show-man. I believe we'll hit record ratings with this episode."

Thomas looked over at Burt Smellie, wondering if anything he said was sincere. After the woman removed the small cordless mic, he walked right over and stood almost up against the obnoxious host. Thomas towered above him.

"Uh . . . it's just a . . . just a show," Mr. Smellie stammered. He looked around, possibly wondering where security was. He almost fell off his chair as he started panicking. It seemed he was about to call out for help when he noticed Thomas Freeman's hand extended.

"Thank you for having me, sir," Thomas said with his hand still waiting.

"Oh yes, of course," Mr. Smellie said in relief. He reached out and took Thomas's hand and shook mildly.

Thomas smiled and squeezed . . . and squeezed . . . and squeezed harder until several cracks were heard.

"What have you gotten yourself into?"

Glenda Eagle sat in her car and stared down the narrow road into the darkness, the path her GPS unit was beckoning her to take. Only the light of the half moon gave a glimpse of the structures down that old industrial street on the outskirts of Los Angeles. A once tall chain-link fence surrounded the perimeter on both sides, but the parts of the fence that remained now lay crumpled on the ground. To the left was a seemingly endless row of old warehouse buildings decorated with a mixture of graffiti and vines, the windows now nothing more than jagged remnants looking like vicious teeth in large, square black mouths. On the right were a half dozen old boxcars rusted to train tracks that went nowhere, no doubt home to drifters and homeless people.

Her heart beat faster as she fought back the foreboding creeping into her thoughts and trying to plant roots in her mind. *Think about the payoff*, she thought. *Think about why you're here*. She took a deep breath and navigated her vehicle into the unknown.

Her headlights offered a temporary reprieve from the bleakness, and as long as she kept her eyes focused in front of her, she felt as if she could continue. The ghostly shadows passing by her peripheral vision told a different tale, and she dared not look. Fighting the urge to turn back, she pressed on.

Something moved in front of her. A large dark figure emerged from an old guard shack to her left. It was a man holding up his right hand. As she neared him, she could see that he was Latino, tall, with a shaved head, large mustache, and unshaven chin. He was scary enough without the butt of the pistol announcing its presence above his belt line.

She stopped the car.

"Good evening," the man said in a gruff tone.

Glenda nodded, although it didn't really seem to be a good evening at all.

The man walked around the car looking carefully into each window, shining his flashlight into every crevice. After a full circle, he brought his attention back to the driver. "What's your business here?"

Glenda tried hard to keep her voice from cracking. "I'm here to pick up a case of spinach for Popeye."

The man stepped back with a quick, sharp nod. "Turn left at the next entrance and follow it to the end."

Glenda did as instructed and turned left at the next road. An old sign that read "Keep Out" dangled from its broken metal post. She followed the road toward the end, trying hard to avoid the numerous potholes and debris. As she neared the last warehouse, she could see other cars and a faint glow coming from behind the building. Parking her car in line with the others, she got out and followed the light. It was a clear, humid summer night, and the stars managed to shout their presence away from the smog and lights of downtown.

As she rounded the corner of the building, she saw the source of the light. It was coming from the opening of a large black tent. Several people were standing in line to get in, so she filed in at the back of the line. A young couple dressed in formal wear took their spot in line behind her. Several of the people were well dressed, which surprised Glenda, but she was glad she had borrowed the black dress and high-heeled shoes she now wore. It was also a good thing she had practiced walking in the heels earlier in the day, which proved to be amazingly harder than she thought it would be.

She was a very coordinated woman with the strength of most men, but her calves were killing her from concentrating on walking without falling. She couldn't wait for this to be over so she could shed the girlie wear for jeans and work boots.

"Place everything in the tray," the man at the entrance said. He was also a very large man with a pistol sticking out of his jeans.

Glenda placed her small purse in the tray and started to walk forward. The man tapped her on the arm. When she looked back, he was patting his right ear.

"Oh sorry." Glenda removed her Bluetooth and placed it in the tray with her purse. The man motioned for her to go through the metal detector as he looked inside her purse and saw the three stacks of twenty-dollar bills. He smiled and handed her the purse and phone.

There was a chain-link fence set up in the middle of the tent with one gate on the near side close to the tent entrance. Bleachers adorned the fence on the other three sides and were already nearly full. Glenda saw a bare spot on the top row and squeezed through the seated spectators.

After a few more folks arrived, they closed the entrance to the tent. The man who had directed her through the metal detector proved also to be the emcee. He strolled to the middle of the fenced area.

"Good evening, ladies and gentlemen." His voice was bold and loud. He didn't even need a microphone. "We have four bouts tonight, so get ready for a wild ride."

He's definitely a showman, Glenda thought. She placed the Bluetooth back in her ear and turned it on. Moving her head in different directions, she took in her surroundings.

"What are you doing?"

Glenda looked at the man sitting to her right. He was not dressed in formal wear. He was stocky and wore a stained T-shirt that had once been white. Thinking quickly, she said, "I was wondering why they don't have a hole in the top of this tent for all this smoke." She coughed and waved her hand in front of her face.

The man stared at her for a few seconds, took a huge puff from his cigar, shook his head, and turned his attention back to the makeshift ring.

"The first fight tonight is between two undefeated monsters," the emcee continued.

Glenda scoffed. *Of course they're undefeated, moron*, she thought.

The emcee raised his arms wide above his head. "Weighing in at 105 pounds, let's hear it for Satan's Spawn."

The crowd cheered and clapped as a young man walked into the ring with his massive pit bull on a leash. Glenda clapped and cheered too. The dog was majestic, solid brown with a huge head full of scars. Satan's Spawn pulled on the leash, growling and flashing his fangs to the amusement of those in the stands.

"Now for his opponent," the emcee said. "Weighing in at 98 pounds, give it up for Thor."

Another young man walked into the ring with his pit bull, a beautiful white dog with a million tiny black specks. Like his opponent, his head and face also gave testament to many battles.

"Place your bets," the emcee concluded as he left the ring and the two guys fought to keep their pits at bay.

Please hurry, Glenda thought as the bookies walked through the bleachers collecting bets. "Oh, forty dollars on Satan's Spawn," Glenda said as she handed the guy two twenty-dollar bills. The man wrote out a slip and handed it to her.

Glenda swallowed hard and her anxiety grew. *Please, please, please hurry*, she thought again.

"No more bets," shouted the emcee, now outside of the ring, as the bookies worked their way out of the stands. "Let's get ready to rumble." He took a whistle and put it to his lips.

The two dogs pulled against their restrainers, their lungs heaving as their flesh expanded and contracted around their rib cages, their mouths starting to foam in anticipation.

The whistle sounded and the dog men unleashed their hounds. The two magnificent creatures met in the middle of the ring on their hind legs as their jaws sought out the other's weaknesses. Fur flew in this barbaric display, and the barbarians in formal wear cheered them on.

Glenda closed her eyes and tilted her head downward and said a silent prayer. It was answered. The tent became flooded with flashing red and blue lights.

"You're surrounded," a voice over a megaphone announced. "Come out in single file with your hands above your head. If you have a firearm, hold it high above your head or you will be shot on sight."

Fear and panic gripped the inhabitants of the tent as the two men leashed their dogs. Some thought to escape the police by crawling under the tent in the back, but the officer wasn't bluffing about the tent being surrounded.

Glenda followed the line of spectators out into the opening. The men in charge of the event, including the first one she saw at the guard shack and the two dog men, were placed in police cars and escorted away. The people there to watch and bet on the fights were all loaded into a large police van.

Before Glenda entered, an officer cuffed her, took her phone and bag and put them into a satchel, scanned the bar code on the handcuffs and the satchel, then tossed the evidence to another officer. He grabbed Glenda by the arm, and not gently, and shoved her into the back of the van. Glenda couldn't help but smile, because she didn't even know paddy wagons still existed.

A very uncomfortable thirty minutes passed before they arrived at the police station. Glenda, along with all the other spectators, was taken to a holding cell. It was an open cell with a wide-open stainless-steel commode. The walls were painted cinder blocks with ink scribbles all over them. The room was poorly lit and smelled of urine. The front desk was only about thirty feet away, where police officers went about their duties without even a glance in their direction.

"I want my phone call," one person yelled.

"I want my attorney," yelled another.

The officers ignored them.

Glenda took a seat on a long bench against the back wall of the cell.

"Can you believe this crap?"

She turned to see her old friend in the stained T-shirt.

"You better have a good lawyer," he said.

Glenda shook her head. As she leaned forward to place her head in her hands, her long, curly red hair flowed down, covering most of her face. She was a strikingly handsome woman of Native American descent. Almost six feet tall, her tan and muscular body gave her a formidable appearance in the borrowed black dress.

Everyone looked up as the keys clanged against the tumblers in the door to the cell.

"All right," an officer said. "Who wants to go first?"

Several people raised their hands and jumped to their feet, including the guy beside Glenda.

"You there," the officer yelled. "Let's start with you, honey. Come on, get off your butt."

Glenda looked up and saw the female officer pointing at her. She got up and followed her out and down a long hallway. They passed the fingerprinting table, mug shot area, several smaller offices, and a water cooler. The officer led her to an interrogation room and motioned for her to sit at the table. She then took off her cuffs and left the room.

Several moments passed as Glenda wondered if anyone was behind the one-way mirror. Finally the door opened and Sergeant Marcus Olazaba walked in carrying Glenda's satchel with her Bluetooth and purse. He was a very clean-cut Latino man in his early thirties.

"Do you have any idea how much trouble you're in?" he asked as he placed his fists on the table and stared across at Glenda. "Well, do you?"

Glenda shrugged. "I'm sorry."

The sergeant shook his head. "You are loco. That's what you are. You do know that, right? And for God's sake, take off that stupid wig."

Glenda smiled and pulled off the red wig, revealing her long, straight gray hair. She ran her fingers through the strands where it had been compressed by the wig.

"How do you think I felt," Sergeant Olazaba continued, "to come to work this evening only to have the chief inform me that Miss Glenda Eagle had sent an e-mail saying she was going undercover tonight to a dogfighting event and would be sending us the information and pictures shortly?"

Glenda gritted her teeth. "You told me to let you know about any such events. That's all I was doing."

"No, no," corrected the sergeant. "I said to let us know if you had information, not to take this information and infiltrate the organization yourself. You could have been killed." He opened the satchel and pulled out the Bluetooth. "What if they had discovered this was a camera uploading a live feed to the Internet?" He opened her purse and took one of the stacks of twenty-dollar bills out. "Or what if they had looked more closely and saw these were only ones with a twenty on each side?"

Glenda sat still. She knew rhetorical questions when she heard them and wasn't about to make things worse by answering.

"Are you not even going to answer me?" he snapped.

"I'm sorry," Glenda offered weakly. "If you need to charge me with a crime, I understand. I just couldn't not try to help those dogs."

Sergeant Olazaba started to say something else, but the door to the interrogation room opened. He quickly stood at attention as the chief walked in.

Chief Jackson walked in and sat at the chair across from Glenda. He stared at her with dark eyes and a seriously upset expression. He was physically intimidating even without the expression, a tall, lean, African American police officer with twenty-three years on the force. He sported three gunshot scars: two from the military and one from the line of duty. "Well, well," he said mockingly. "If it ain't Sherlock Holmes. No, wait—James Bond. What in the hell were you thinking?"

Glenda could only shrug her shoulders.

"You're lucky we don't throw you under the jail." It wasn't an original line, but effective. He looked at the sergeant. "Should we throw the book at her, Sarge?"

"Yes, sir. I think we should. But she'd probably just throw it back."

The chief didn't even crack a smile, just continued to stare at her.

"Can I say something?" Glenda asked.

"No!" they both shouted.

The chief finally got up and walked to the door. As he opened it, he turned to leave a few parting words. "If I ever read an e-mail like that from you again, I'll . . . I'll . . . Well, I better not ever receive an e-mail like that from you again. Am I clear?"

Glenda nodded. "Yes, sir."

One last glance up at the sergeant and the chief walked out.

Sergeant Olazaba shook his head and sat in the chair across from her, the same chair the chief had just vacated. "Look, I know you love these dogs. So do I. I admire all the good you do for them up at your rescue. I just don't want to see anything happen to you. What would all your dogs do without you?"

Glenda hadn't even looked at it from that point of view. Her shelter, the Pit Stop, stayed maxed out at almost one thousand pit bulls. She knew each one personally and loved each one uniquely. "You're right," she said. "It was foolish. Next time I'll give you the information."

The sergeant looked at her with disbelief, then laughed. "We better leave it on that note. I don't think you've ever agreed with me before. Now go on, get the heck out of here and go home."

3

"Shark!"

Erique Sarpong and his fourteen-year-old son, Emmanuel, stared across the small wooden table for a full second before dropping their playing cards and running to the back of the boat, both of their folding chairs tumbling to the deck. This was the general direction of the scream, but no one was visible, so they weren't sure who had called out.

Five years ago, when the tourist industry began to boom in North Africa, Erique had converted his fishing operation along the crowded beaches of Nouakchott, the capital of Mauritania, into a charter business, taking rich foreign tourists out scuba diving. He cleaned up his old twenty-five-foot boat, added a fresh coat of paint, refinished the decking, and gave her a name: *The Blue Horizon*. It proved to be a smart move, as the money he made doing this far outweighed what he squeezed out of the local fish market. It was much easier work, and he could actually take days off to enjoy time with his family. But in all those years, this was the first time he had ever heard this word.

"Where are they, Papa?"

Erique scanned the surface of the water, the small swells rocking the boat gently. He stepped over the transom and onto the diving platform that he had built and added to his boat. Bracing himself with one hand on the large outboard motor, he squatted down as if trying to peer into the sea, his strong, thin frame flexing the muscles beneath his dark skin, which reflected in the bright sunshine. Beads of sweats began falling from his shaved head. "I don't know. Keep your eyes open."

A hand breached the surface twenty feet behind the boat. Without thinking, Erique dove in and began to swim toward the diver. As he neared the person, he could taste the blood in the water. He grabbed on to the diver's hands and pulled them to him. The diver panicked and tried to use Erique, who was not wearing a life jacket, as a flotation device. Luckily Erique was a strong swimmer and managed to keep them both above water and began swimming back toward the boat. He wasn't sure, but he thought he felt something brush against his leg.

Emmanuel, still in a state of shock himself, wiped the tears from his eyes and grabbed the foam lifesaver, climbed over the transom, and threw it out in their direction while holding on to the attached rope. As his father latched on, he pulled them quickly to the boat and helped his father get the diver onto the platform. It was the woman diver.

"Where is your husband?" Erique asked as the woman climbed over into the boat and collapsed onto the deck.

She took off her mask, the fear still clearly visible in her eyes. "I don't know. We were not together. A shark came out of nowhere and hit me from behind. I never saw it." She didn't look at Erique when she spoke. She didn't appear to be speaking to anyone in particular.

As Erique helped her remove the gear, he noticed the air line coming from her tank had been severed. Then he noticed the blood cascading down her wet suit into his boat. "You're bleeding. Did the shark bite you?"

The woman didn't respond. Her eyes were now void of understanding, as if Erique were not speaking English.

"Keep an eye out for the husband," Erique instructed his son as he started running his hands over the woman's shoulders, arms, and back, searching for a wound. As he caressed the back of her left arm, she grimaced in pain. He lifted her arm, looked around, and saw the bite mark. It had penetrated the wet suit, and several punctures seemed to be pretty deep. He got up and went to the controls of the boat and retrieved the first-aid kit. "Help her take the stuff off," he said to Emmanuel.

Emmanuel did as his father instructed. As he began to help her off with the suit, he looked out over the water. "Papa, there he is."

Erique followed the direction of his son's finger and saw the other diver, the woman's husband, swimming on the surface about fifty feet off the starboard side. He appeared to be fine, so Erique squatted down again to see to the woman's wound.

"Look!" Emmanuel yelled. "Dolphins."

Erique breathed a sigh of relief. If the shark was still around, the dolphins would protect the diver still in the water. As he began to clean the bite wound, however, he was shocked. It was not a shark bite. The puncture wounds indicated a much narrower jawline than a shark. *Maybe a barracuda?* he thought. No, it wasn't a barracuda either, but there was something familiar about the shape of the bite.

"How is she?" Emmanuel asked as he knelt down beside them.

Erique continued to cleanse the wound and then began to apply a bandage.

"That's not a shark bite, is it?" his son asked.

Suddenly it became clear as a rush of fear and disbelief overcame Erique. He stood up and stared out at the diver swimming toward them but still thirty feet away. He could see three dorsal fins from the dolphins to the diver's left and two more approaching from the right. They were closing in fast.

"Start the boat," he said.

Emmanuel heard but was frozen as it also dawned on him what was happening. He looked back at the woman's wound and then at the dolphins who were heading straight for the diver. They were not going to be of assistance. As they neared, one by one, they sped up and rammed the diver.

"Help!" the diver cried out.

"Start the boat," Erique ordered again.

25

Emmanuel rushed to the front and turned the key. The engine sputtered once and expelled a plume of smoke as it came to life. He put it in gear and turned toward the diver to close the distance. He could see the dolphins still attacking, but he heard no more cries from the diver.

Erique stepped onto the platform again as the boat neared the motionless black form in the water. As the boat passed, he grabbed the diver and pulled him up onto the platform. "Help me!" he yelled.

Emmanuel ran to the rear and helped pull the limp body over the transom. It hit the deck with a thud as water and blood flooded the floor. As his father lifted one leg over, he screamed out in pain. Emmanuel looked over and couldn't believe his eyes. A dolphin had come out of the water and was biting his father, its jaws clamped tight to Erique's ankle. Emmanuel looked around for a weapon but saw nothing, so he leaned over and began punching the dolphin with his fist. He could see more approaching. He punched harder as his father held on to the back of the boat and began kicking at the dolphin with his free foot. Finally it released its grip and slid back into the murky water.

They both collapsed beside the diver's body. Erique ignored his own wounds to check the diver's condition. It seemed pretty obvious that he was dead. He looked over to the wife but she was still in shock, her eyes staring into a void where reality wasn't invited.

How was he going to explain this to the authorities? Would they even believe him? He looked to his son for strength, but what he saw was pure fear. Emmanuel's eyes were staring out over the water. It caused a sensation like needle pricks igniting and cascading down his spine in a chain reaction. He jumped to his feet and looked out over the water to where his son was staring. He saw them—two large whales coming directly toward them. They were huge, humpbacks maybe.

He ran to the controls and started the boat and gave it full throttle. He headed due east back toward home as fast as the boat would go. Dolphins followed and swam alongside for a while. Finally they disappeared, and there was nothing but water as far as the eye could see. He scanned the boat and saw the woman still staring straight ahead as if in a trance, her breathing fast but consistent. He saw the diver in the back still lying in a pool of blood. He saw his son sitting in one of the folding chairs, his bare feet resting in the bloody water, his face buried in his hands and crying uncontrollably.

What just happened? He grabbed the transmitter from its holder beside the steering wheel. "Mayday! Mayday! We have an emergency."

The radio buzzed and crackled. "This is the coast guard. What is the nature of your emergency?"

"This is Erique Sarpong of *The Blue Horizon*. I have two divers that have been attacked. Need emergency assistance."

"What is the nature of the attacks?"

Erique looked back at the divers. He couldn't bring himself to say. "Unknown. One diver is unconscious and the other is losing blood. Can you send a helicopter?"

"Negative," came the reply. "It's on another rescue mission. What is your destination and ETA? We will have medics waiting for you there."

Erique squeezed the transmitter handle. "We are headed back to Nouakchott. Should be there in just over an hour."

"Affirmative."

The radio went silent. Erique stood there holding the transmitter, afraid to let go of the one link to the rest of the world. Finally he placed it back in its holder and called out to his son. "Emmanuel! Emmanuel!"

His son slowly looked up.

"Come and take the wheel, son."

He did as he was instructed, and Erique went back to check the bandages of the female diver. The male diver lay face down in six inches of water, so there was no doubt of his condition. Still, Erique sat him up in a less obvious position and went back to the controls.

It was the longest hour of his life. At last he saw the beach

27

and the flashing lights of the emergency vehicle at the beach end of the public pier. It would have been much easier to use the fishing docks, and less crowded, but he was just glad to see the paramedics. He made a beeline for them and pulled his boat up as quickly as he dared to the end of the pier.

The paramedics hurried and climbed down the ladder into his boat and checked both divers. A man with dark-brown slacks and a light-brown shirt came aboard also. He wore a badge on his chest. He was tall and slim with very dark skin, much like Erique's. He watched the paramedics very carefully. After they had carried the divers out of the boat and secured them in the ambulance, he walked around the small boat as if looking for clues. He took the clipboard down from the dash and read over it, then replaced it. After making a second trip around the boat, he turned his attention to Erique.

"This is your boat, sir?"

Erique nodded. "Yes, sir. I am Erique Sarpong. This is my son, Emmanuel."

The man looked at his son then back to him. "I am Jakande. I need you to come with me to the police station so you can tell me what happened." Then he noticed the blood running down Erique's heel. "Or do you need to go to the hospital?"

"No, I'm fine." Erique threw a quick bandage on his foot and put his shoe over it. Then he looked at Emmanuel. "Take the boat back and make sure you put everything away. Tell your mama I'll be home as soon as I can."

"Yes, Papa."

Erique grabbed his clipboard by the radio and followed the officer up the ladder, and they walked side by side to where the pier met the beach. When they reached the officer's car, Erique opened the back door.

"No, no. Sit up here," the officer said.

Erique felt a little better not riding in the back. Once they arrived at the police station, he followed the officer inside past several desks until they came to a small office.

Officer Jakande sat behind the desk and motioned for Erique to take the seat across from the desk, the only other seat there.

Erique sat and looked around the office. The blinds were so dirty that sunlight barely penetrated. A small ceiling fan churned overhead, the crud so caked up on the blades that itthey appeared as part of the unit. The light dangling from the fan had no cover and gyrated with the rotation of the blades. It looked as if it hadn't been cleaned since . . . well, since it was installed. Papers adorned every wall and were piled at least a foot high on the floor. There was one old file cabinet that appeared to be rusted closed. The top of this was also covered in stacks of papers.

The officer took out a blank form. "Who were the divers?"

Erique handed him the clipboard with the charter agreement. The officer copied down the names and contact information for the couple.

"When did they reserve your boat, Mr. Sarpong?"

"About two months ago," Erique said.

"Have they hired you before?" the officer asked.

"No, this was the first time."

"Okay, Mr. Sarpong, tell me what happened."

Erique took a deep breath and told the officer the entire story. The officer sat there expressionless, leaning back in his chair with his hands cupped behind his head as he took it all in.

"You expect me to believe that?" the officer asked after Erique finished.

"I don't know, sir. I'm not even sure I believe it. But I'm telling you what I saw."

The officer studied him for several seconds until the phone on his desk rang. He let it ring three times before picking it up. "Jakande. Yes, go ahead please." He listened carefully for a few moments before thanking the caller and hanging up. "That was the hospital. The man is dead. Cause of death was a result of being hit many times to the abdomen."

Erique swallowed hard.

"The woman is in stable condition and they've treated the bite wound on her arm. The doctor said you probably saved her life with the first-aid treatment."

Erique bowed his head and exhaled deeply. At least that was good news.

"Why do you think they did this?" the officer asked.

"Who? Did what?"

"The dolphins," the officer said. "Do you think maybe they had a baby in the pod and the divers got too close?"

Erique breathed a sigh of relief. That was the first indication that the officer believed his story. "It could have been. I didn't see one, but it might be the answer."

"I say it's the heat."

"What do you mean?" Erique asked.

The officer picked up an inch-thick manila folder on his desk. "Every year it gets hotter and every year the amount of violent crime increases. This godforsaken heat drives people mad. If it has that effect on humans, why not creatures like dolphins and whales? I read once that they have almost the same intelligence as we do."

"You really think it's possible?"

The officer nodded. "Why do you think the helicopter wasn't available? It was rescuing a family in a sailboat about ten miles south of you being attacked by two killer whales."

4

"Advance!" Colonel Benjamin Jamison waved his arm slowly as he gave the order. He stood watching his soldiers make their way forward. Colonel Jamison stood firm, his broad shoulders making him look taller than he was. Beads of sweat ran slowly down his shaved head. He looked back at his radioman, an African American like himself, and nodded.

His troops started walking slowly through the thick undergrowth of the jungle, their rifles at the ready. The air was dense and hard to inhale. The leaves were damp from the earlier rain. The humidity seemed to be an entity of its own and on the enemy's side.

The sky above, barely visible through the tree canopy, was overcast in a brilliant array of colors and seemed to be swirling in a counterclockwise motion. Large flying insects high above the jungle floor mimicked the motion as they flew in swirls as well.

The trees themselves were huge, with some trunks eight feet in diameter. All of the trees seemed to have the same structured limb formation with huge branches coming out both sides and then turning ninety degrees upward, as if signaling the soldiers to stop.

Every soldier moved slowly with eyes darting back and forth, trying to peer into the limited distance the heavy foliage provided. They all knew the enemy was out there—waiting.

Colonel Jamison could see the fear in the eyes of the combat men and women on either side of him. He tried to offer a reassuring smile, but the fact was that his heart was beating abnormally fast. He had a very bad feeling.

"Sir," his radioman said, "I can't hear anything."

Colonel Jamison grabbed the radio and held it to his ear. At first he couldn't hear anything either, then a very low sound began to emerge, then louder. It was the voices of their enemy. He tried hard to understand it but couldn't understand one word. He handed the radio back to the soldier.

An explosion went off somewhere, then another and another. Gunfire erupted.

"Hit the ground!" the colonel yelled.

Bullets and tracers ripped the air above his head as he crawled on his belly toward the source of the insurgency. The weeds were so high he could no longer see his men, but he could hear their return fire. He squinted and stared through the plant life but could see nothing to shoot at. Water dripped from large leaves onto his face. Bugs buzzed by his ears.

He jumped up and unloaded his entire clip toward the direction they had been walking and quickly fell back to the ground. Gunfire and explosions grew louder and louder, until . . . it all stopped. No guns, no explosions, nothing.

The colonel stood up and looked around. There were no sounds. No sounds of war and no sounds of animals. He looked upward and saw no flying insects, and the sun pierced through the treetops. He shielded his eyes and looked around. Everything seemed different. He listened for any sounds. Silence. Even his radioman was gone.

"Where did everyone go, Daddy?"

Colonel Jamison looked down beside him and couldn't believe what he saw. "Victoria? What are you doing here? You shouldn't be here, honey."

His four-year-old daughter was there wearing her Sunday dress. Her hair was up in pigtails and she was smiling. "I wanted to be with you, Daddy."

He knelt beside his daughter and returned the smile. "I want that too, sweetheart. I want that more than anything. But it's not safe here."

At that moment an explosion lifted them both off the ground and threw them in different directions.

"Victoria!" he screamed. "Where are you?"

"I'm over here."

The colonel looked toward the sound of the tiny voice and panicked. "No! No! Get away from there."

Victoria looked at her dad as if she didn't understand and began to walk down the steps into the swimming pool. The water began to get deeper and deeper. Then only her head remained visible; the rest of her body was submerged in the dark water.

Colonel Jamison tried to rush to her, but couldn't move. Vines were wrapped tightly around his ankles preventing him from going to his daughter.

Her head slowly began to disappear under the surface.

"No!" he screamed.

Missiles started hitting the jungle all around him. No, not missiles, but red laser beams, it seemed. They were coming from the sky. "What's going on?" the colonel asked aloud to himself. "Is it drones? Run, Victoria, run!"

Suddenly the enemy advanced. They ran through the jungle with ease, carrying their massive weapons with them. But they weren't human; they were monsters. They looked like ogres or trolls the colonel had seen in horror movies.

The colonel managed to get to his feet as one of the monsters approached. He looked all around but couldn't see his daughter or the swimming pool anymore. He tried to fire his rifle but it wouldn't fire. He searched for grenades, something with which to defend himself, but couldn't find anything.

As the creature lunged for him, Angel came to the rescue. She leaped into the air and started biting the monster in the face. The monster swung wildly but could not get away from his attacker. A laser beam hit exactly where they were standing, creating a sonic boom, and everything went black.

The colonel sat up quickly as he regained consciousness, his breathing rushing in and out of his lungs, cold sweat tickling his face. He looked around but it was dark. Finally things started to come into focus. He could see a red light with numbers beside him. He could see a faint light coming underneath the door. He could see the form of his wife sleeping beside him.

He reached over and turned on the light. The sheets and pillowcase on his side were soaking wet. He was glad his dream had not awoken his wife. He slid his legs off the bed and tried to rub the sleep from his eyes.

Angel, his pit bull, sat at the side of the bed staring up at him. She was solid white with a pink nose with matching ears.

"Thanks for waking me," the colonel whispered. He noticed the time was six thirty and decided to go ahead and get up for the day. It was a Saturday and he didn't have to work, but having been a military man most of his life, he was accustomed to not sleeping late.

After a shower, he went to the kitchen to start the coffeemaker and put two bagels in the toaster. Retrieving the newspaper from his front steps, he sat at the table and began to read. It was always the same: politicians pointing fingers, record heat waves, and peace still holding in the Middle East. The colonel nodded at that news. He had been involved in the last war, which ranged all over the Middle East, and ended with peace talks ten years ago in 2040. As a soldier, he loved to read about peace in the world.

"All right, girl," he said to Angel, "come on." He walked to the back door and opened it, and Angel slowly walked out. He watched as she circled the perimeter along the privacy fence, sniffing as she went. The grass in the backyard was brown with patches of dirt beginning to dot the landscape. He so wished he could turn on the sprinklers, but there was a statewide ban on that right now.

He walked over and looked at the patio thermometer. It was already ninety degrees and not even seven thirty yet. He looked at the two shriveled vines in the rectangular planter. His two tomato plants never had a chance and burned up before they could mature. He looked up at the bright sky and wondered if he would ever be able to produce a garden again. He missed the fresh vegetables he used to be able to grow.

The colonel had been stationed here in Georgia for the last two years, and even though he was raised in the South, he didn't remember it being this unbearably hot and humid. "Come on, girl; let's not stay out here too long." Angel trotted to the door and entered with the colonel close behind. He took his seat again at the table.

"Good morning. Why didn't you wake me?"

He looked up to see his wife, Belinda, enter the dining room wearing her bathrobe and drying her hair. She sat at the table beside him and grabbed a bagel. She was nearing sixty years old but still looked amazingly young. Her complexion was soft and smooth, and her smile was as brilliant as it had been when they got married.

"You were sleeping so peacefully. I didn't want to disturb you."

She smiled. "Anything in the news?"

"Same old, same old," he said and slid the paper to her. "You want some eggs this morning?"

"Eggs would be nice."

The colonel walked to the refrigerator and took out the eggs. He almost dropped them before getting them to the counter. He took a deep breath and tried to get his fingers to stop shaking. He set the eggs down and turned on the eye of the stove. As he fumbled for the right pan, his wife walked up behind him.

"Let me do this. You sit and rest."

He obeyed the orders and returned to the table. He stared at his hands as if they were the culprit. "I'm getting old," he said. "Old and useless."

"You had the dream again, didn't you?" Belinda asked with sad eyes. "I noticed the sheets."

He nodded. "Yes, I did. Why can't I have a recurring dream about being stranded on a tropical island surrounded by a hundred beautiful young women?"

His wife chuckled. "Because then I'd be waking you."

The colonel smiled but it faded quickly.

"Exactly the same as always?" she asked.

The colonel thought about the monsters in the dream and chuckled. "No, not the same this time. It had a weird twist." Remembering the other odd thing about the dream, he looked down at Angel and patted her on the head. "Several weird things."

Angel loved the attention and licked his hand to show it. She was getting up there in years for a dog, thirteen years to be exact. The colonel had gotten her as a puppy and took her to war with him ten years ago, a decision that would always haunt him as he endlessly wondered if Angel had been home, maybe his daughter wouldn't have fallen into the swimming pool and drowned.

Belinda set a plate of eggs and bacon in front of him and retook her seat with a plate of her own. "So it was really different this time? Your dream? What do you think that means?"

The colonel laughed. He knew where his wife was going. She loved everything to do with the supernatural. "It doesn't mean anything, except maybe I'm going crazy. But you already know that."

"Ben, you know it's a proven fact that people can have dreams that give them a glimpse into the future. I've read about it."

"Proven?" The colonel smiled. "Just because someone with letters after their name said it doesn't make it fact."

Belinda sipped her coffee. "You should believe in premonition."

"Well, I don't," he said. "But I have this strange feeling someday I will." He chuckled at his joke even though he had told it a hundred times.

His wife rolled her eyes. She looked down at Angel, who still sat at the colonel's feet with a look of anticipation. "At least you're still sane, aren't you, girl?"

The colonel put his dish in the sink and walked to the living room, sat in his recliner, and turned on the TV.

"Is that your plans for today?" she asked.

"Affirmative." He turned it straight to the news.

The screen displayed a map of the United States, and the female newscaster was motioning with one hand and holding a stack of papers with the other. "At least thirty-eight states will experience record high temperatures today," she said. "If you live in the southern states, a heat advisory is in effect until 7:00 p.m. tonight. Do not leave pets outdoors, and make sure to drink plenty of water."

The colonel's wife came into the living room and sat to watch.

The newswoman continued. "Do not leave pets inside cars, not even to run into the store for a minute. A catastrophe was averted yesterday when a woman left two dogs in her car at Perimeter Mall. As the temperature neared dangerous levels, one of the dogs, a pit bull named Roger Dodger, took matters into his own hands by breaking the driver's-side window and freeing himself and his Chihuahua brother."

The colonel looked down at his feet at Angel and wondered how people could be so careless with their pets.

"The hot weather is not just affecting us here; it's also having an effect on fishermen. Let's go live to the Gulf." The scene changed to one with an ocean background. Another reporter, this one a young man, was holding a microphone and standing next to a beautiful Asian woman.

"Thanks, Andrea," the male reporter said. "I'm here with Sally Xie, who is a marine biologist. Dr. Xie, can you tell us what is happening to the water temps?"

Sally nodded. "The water temps have become unpredictable. We're experiencing record highs all around the globe, and so far there is no pattern to explain why certain areas of the world's oceans are getting hotter than others."

"And how does this affect the fishing industry?"

"In a very bad way," Sally said. "Shrimp need cooler waters just to survive. Shrimp fishers are having to go to deeper waters to find them, but aren't having much luck. Plankton cannot thrive in warm waters, and if the plankton disappear, it causes a chain reaction. The crustaceans that feed on the plankton disappear, along with the smaller fish that feed on the crustaceans, and the bigger fish that feed on them."

"It sounds pretty serious," the reporter said. "How can this be fixed?"

Sally shrugged. "I truly don't know. I don't know if it can be fixed. I think we have to determine if this is simply a natural planetary cycle, or if in fact humans are causing it. Either way, we can't do anything until we know the cause."

"Are there any other problems being caused by the heat?"

"Yes," Sally said, looking directly into the camera. "There has been a behavioral change in the sea life as well."

The reporter looked at the camera, then back to Sally. "What do you mean?"

"Well, for starters, the migration for many of the larger whale species we monitor is very erratic. And many of the mammals, such as porpoises, have begun to show aggression never before documented. This might be due to the diminishing food supply. It might be just competition and survival of the fittest. We simply don't know."

"Well, Andrea," the reporter said, looking back into the camera, "it doesn't look good. My advice: stay out of the water. Back to you."

The colonel muted the television. "You don't have to tell me twice. I'm not going anywhere near the ocean."

"Like you ever did," his wife joked.

"It sure is hot, ain't it, boy?" Darren Mitchell switched hands with the leash and plastic bag of groceries he was carrying. He lifted his hand with the plastic bag to his forehead and wiped away the excess beads of sweat. He nodded to the few people he saw on the street, even though he didn't speak Spanish. Well, his last and only girlfriend did teach him one line so he could, in her words, explain anything to her family. The line was "*Yo soy blanco*," which means "I am white."

Truer words were never spoken. He was a short, thin fellow with a severely receded hairline for a man in his early thirties. What little hair remained was red, very red, and he sunburned easily. Even for this short trip he used an entire bottle of sunscreen and wore his oversized Atlanta Braves ball cap. There was hardly a square inch of his arms and bald head that wasn't freckled.

A physicist and comic book buff, he was the newest administrator of the SETI complex about two miles out of El Triunfo, a small village near the southern border of Mexico on the edge of the Sierra Madre. He had been there only a week and the stored-up supplies were running low. There was a small truck there for emergencies, but it seemed like such a nice day, he decided to walk Roscoe to town. The sweat ring across the front of his shirt testified to the fact that he wished he had brought the truck.

His pit bull, Roscoe, didn't slow down or look around. He was happy that they were out walking. This was only the second time they had come into town at all. Roscoe was a very large brown-and-white pit bull, weighing over eighty pounds, who loved everyone, people and animals alike. Darren had found him living in the wild in

39

Alabama on a trip visiting his parents. His tail and ears had been cut, and he looked rather vicious, albeit undernourished. He was living in a wooded area full of coyotes—and surviving. Of course, now he looked like a coyote would be a snack for him.

Darren had not actually been looking for a dog at that point in his life, especially not a full-grown pit bull, and he had tried to explain to his parents that he didn't have the time or the room for a dog right then, but they were relentless. So he brought the scrawny, filthy mongrel home with him, and it was the best decision he ever made. Roscoe was the best dog he ever met and he loved him dearly.

He neared the last building in town where the dirt road turned to go toward the SETI radio astronomy lab, which rested inside a fenced encasement. On the top of the building was the large satellite dish used to scan the heavens for any faint sign of a signal not from this world. As he turned down the side of the building, however, he almost stopped. There were five young men dressed in what appeared to be gang clothes.

Roscoe kept walking without a care in the world until the young men stepped in front of him. Roscoe looked back to Darren.

"Hey, *güey*," the leader said. "Where you going?"

Darren removed his rim glasses and wiped away the perspiration. "Oh, hey fellows. We're just headed back to the lab."

Another of the young men laughed. "Yeah, man, he's the one out there looking for aliens.

Can you believe that?"

"You don't like aliens, *güey*?" the leader asked. "What's your problem with aliens? My uncle was an alien and you arrested him in America."

"It wasn't me," Darren said weakly and tried to walk on by.

The leader grabbed Roscoe's collar. "Are you dissing me? Did I say you could go? This here is my street. You want to use my street and not even take a little time to be friendly?"

"That's a nice pit bull," another of the gang said.

The leader patted Roscoe on the head. "Yeah, he a big boy all

40

right. He likes to go for walks, eh?"

Darren nodded. "Yes, he does."

The leader began to run his hand up the leash. "Tell you what, alien hunter, we're gonna do you a solid. We love dogs. We'll take him for a walk for you and bring him back to your place when we're finished. How about that?"

"He's already tired," Darren said. "I'll just take him home."

"*Mande?*" the leader snapped. "Did you hear this *sangrón?*"

The others began to laugh.

"Just give me the leash. I'll treat him like he was my own dog. Don't worry; we'll bring him to you when we're finished."

Darren stood fast and held firm.

The leader's eyes squinted. "Let me make it clear, little man." He raised his shirt to reveal his pistol. "You understand now?" He pulled on the leash but Darren wouldn't let go.

"You gonna die for this mutt, man?" one of the others asked.

Darren didn't know what to say. He was scared to death, but he couldn't bring himself to let go of Roscoe's leash. He knew it would be the last time he ever saw him.

The leader suddenly jerked the leash and it leaped out of Darren's hand, leaving a rope burn in its departure. He started walking off with Roscoe in tow. Roscoe looked back toward Darren as if wondering what was going on. Darren took a step toward them, but two of the gang members stood in front of them.

One pulled a switchblade knife. "Don't even think it," he said.

The other reached down and yanked the plastic bag of groceries out of Darren's other hand. "We probably gonna need this to feed your dog while we watching him for you."

The two laughed as they joined the exodus.

Darren couldn't believe what was happening. He thought of rushing them but feared he'd get them both killed. The moment was surreal. He wasn't sure if it was real or a heat-induced hallucination. Was he about to lose his beloved Roscoe forever?

He started walking toward the gang. "Hey, I can't let you take my dog," he yelled.

The leader turned around, apparently out of patience. He reached down and caressed his weapon. The rest of the group turned around also, and all of them began walking back toward Darren. As they got within five feet of him, they all stopped. The leader removed his hand from the pistol and stared past Darren. All of them seemed to be looking beyond him.

Darren heard a noise and turned to look in the direction of the stares. An older Chevrolet Impala had turned down the alley and was slowly approaching them. It pulled all the way up to Darren and stopped.

Another Mexican man got out. A faint mustache and goatee accentuated his taut young face. He was short and thin, with dark eyes and olive skin. He wore a sleeveless shirt, and his arms displayed several tattoos, among which were satanic symbols. "What's going on?" he asked.

"Nothing that concerns you, Francisco," the gang leader answered in a friendly tone.

"They're stealing my dog," Darren blurted out.

Nobody moved for several seconds. Finally Francisco walked right up to the gang leader, took the leash from his hands, and walked Roscoe over to Darren. As his back was turned, the leader's face turned beet red and his hand once against found its way to the pistol tucked into his jeans.

"You sure you want to do that?' Francisco asked without looking around.

The leader laughed and threw his hands up. "*Chido*. It's all good."

With that they all turned and walked away.

As they turned the corner out of sight, Darren finally breathed a sigh of relief. He looked around to thank his rescuer and smiled. Francisco was on his knees getting kisses from a grateful Roscoe. "What's your name, big boy?"

"He's Roscoe."

"That's a good name," Francisco said.

"Thank you, my friend. You just saved our lives," Darren said.

Francisco stood up. "Are you loco? What are you doing here?" Darren explained his job.

"Then stay out there. Some people here are not too fond of outsiders." Francisco started to walk away.

"Thanks again for saving us," Darren offered.

"They didn't want to kill you," Francisco explained. "They wanted your dog to sell for fighting or breeding."

"He's been neutered."

Francisco shrugged. "That don't matter. He's got good genes. They can use him for cloning more fighting dogs."

Darren realized his other hand was empty. "Oh shoot. They took my groceries."

Francisco walked over and took a pen from Darren's pocket protector and wrote on a small piece of paper. "Here; this is my aunt's store. Tell her I gave you the number and she'll have someone deliver the stuff to you."

Darren thanked him again and watched him drive away. Then he got himself and Roscoe out of town as quickly as possible. When he got back to the lab, he unlocked the gate and then the front door to the two-story block building. It was almost like a fortress, so he wasn't too worried about them trying to mess with him here.

Turning on the lights, he let Roscoe loose and the dog ran straight to the water dish. Likewise, Darren rushed to the refrigerator and pulled out a cold bottled water. He turned it up and finished it without stopping.

After a shower and change of clothes, he prepared Roscoe's dinner and fed him. Then he checked out the printout from the spectrum analyzer. "No calls," he said jokingly.

Roscoe looked up, then returned to eating.

"Aliens are so rude," Darren continued with the joke, possibly because he was still shook up from the earlier events.

After he ate his own dinner that night, he checked all the instruments before going to bed. "Let's try something fun tonight, Roscoe. Let's do a three-sixty scan." Darren entered the commands into the computer. The huge dish on the roof began to move slowly, causing a creaking noise as the static friction of the giant cogs came to life, then settled into a dull hum.

Darren climbed into bed with a comic book. Roscoe jumped over him to take his place on the back side of the small twin bed. Between the walk earlier, the reading, and the moan of the giant dish above them, Darren was soon fast asleep.

Several hours passed as Darren dreamed of little green men. Suddenly he was awoken by Roscoe barking ferociously. He jumped out of bed and fumbled for the light switch, thinking the gang members had come calling. But Roscoe was not barking at anything on the outside; he was concentrating solely on the large speaker beside the computer screen.

"What is it, you crazy dog?" Darren tried to get him to come back to bed, but it was clear something had spooked him. "Wait a minute. Did you hear something? Is that it?"

Darren looked at the printout. Nada. There were no peaks or spikes on the computer screen, just the low fluctuating line that represented normal static noise. Darren sat in front of the computer and looked at his dog. "You did hear something, didn't you?" He stopped the rotation of the dish and programmed it to go back the way it had come. He sat there several minutes listening.

"I must be crazy," Darren said and got up to make a cup of instant coffee. "But of course I knew that when I chose this profession." He sat back down and turned up the cup to his mouth, then almost choked as Roscoe started barking again.

"What?" Darren stared at the screen and placed the earphone on his head. Nothing. Then he saw a very thin line appear and disappear on the screen. "Wait. What was that?" He adjusted the dish to go back. There it was again. He stopped the dish.

Could it be? he thought. It was so faint that he could not hear it, but the screen was clearly picking up a weak signal.

He located the area of space where it seemed to be coming from and began the painful task of cross-checking all known sources from satellites and quasars. It didn't match anything. He looked at the time—3:35 a.m. He signed on to the computer and pulled up his list of all known SETI observation sites in the world and e-mailed them all the coordinates.

"Holy moly," came the e-mail back from Sydney, Australia. "Is this real?"

Soon other locations were chiming in with the same excitement, and before long, they were all referencing the "Mitchell Signal."

At six o'clock that morning, there was a pounding on the door. Darren was still so excited he didn't even think and simply flung open the door. It was his boss.

"Well, are you going to invite me in?"

Darren laughed and stuck out his hand. "Of course, Dr. De Luca. Please come in."

Dr. Vincent De Luca was an older gentleman but kept his thick hair and mustache dyed jet black, perhaps in an attempt to retain his youth. He was shorter than Darren, only five feet even, and walked with a serious limp. No one had ever asked why. He wore his standard work clothes: an older brown corduroy suit with a bright-red bow tie.

Roscoe barked for attention as the two SETI guys sat down to compare notes.

"So that's how it works, Darren? I send you down here to get rid of you and in only two weeks you make the discovery of the millennium?"

Darren blushed and nodded.

"Well," his boss said, "people have been working on this for the last two hours. Tell me what has been learned."

Darren opened a manila folder and began to read. "It's definitely not a star or satellite. It has a mathematical repetition that repeats itself every two hundred twenty-seven seconds. The signal is directed toward the oceans."

"The oceans?" his boss interrupted. "Why the oceans?"

Darren shrugged. "We don't know. But the signal has actually been around for years. We've just now discovered it. But several other dish locations have gone back through records to search the same area that the signal is coming from and have found evidence of it."

"How is it we never heard it before?" his boss asked.

"It's too faint. You can't detect it with the human ear. They've had to find times when certain dishes were tuned to this area, feed them through an amplifier, then break down the recordings into digital conversions."

"Then how did you—" his boss began.

Darren smiled and pointed to Roscoe.

His boss laughed. "You're kidding. Maybe we need to put dogs in all the stations. Well, like I said, kid, this is the biggest thing to ever happen and you're going to be in on everything. Who knows where this will lead."

Darren stopped smiling. "There's something else."

"What?" Dr. De Luca asked, seeing the seriousness on Darren's face.

"We've determined that the signal is continuing to increase in strength. The results from today are definitely more pronounced than those three years ago."

His boss considered the ramifications. "So you're saying the signal is getting louder?"

"No, sir. Not louder—closer."

"It's like talking to a group of kindergartners," one woman said.

"Worse," the other replied. "I've spoken to kids in kindergarten and had better results."

"Good point," the first woman agreed. "I mean, seriously, what's the purpose of preparing all of this information if they're not even going to believe it?"

"Exactly. How insulting was that? I wanted to slap the guy from Georgia."

Dr. Stephen McNair sat on the bench and watched the two women walk past him carrying briefcases. They had just left the same room he would be entering, and they had addressed the same people he would be addressing, the same people who had aggravated these women so successfully. Other pedestrians filled the long hallway, and it dawned on him he should probably stop staring at the tight-fitting dresses around the gracious curves of the women walking away.

He looked at the floor and waited to be called. He sat motionless, his breathing heavy, like a man sitting in a sauna filling his lungs with hot, stagnant air. His belly formed a round pooch that interrupted the skinny construction of his tall, slender frame.

The dimly lit corridor was void of decorations and seemed like a tomb to Dr. McNair. His collar was itchy and uncomfortable as his hands rested on a copy of his report, the report that had already been provided to members of the Congressional Oversight Committee. He hated addressing Congress, and he knew the findings of his latest report would spark the inevitable childish arguments from these top political figures.

He took his handkerchief and wiped away a bead of sweat from his pale forehead. His salt-and-pepper hair showed the signs of the last two missed barbershop appointments and hadn't yet seen a comb today. It might have looked in style for a kid, but on an older man it was just messy. He wore a light-blue button-up shirt with short sleeves, khaki pants, and a navy-blue sweater vest. Had he remembered that today was the day he was supposed to come here, he might have added a tie. Of course he never wore one to work, so why would he wear one here? This was work after all.

Often he had regretted taking this government-funded job and missed the expeditions that working for MIT had allowed. He wished for one more adventure outside the office before he retired, but the possibilities of that looked bleak. Now he spent all his time in a lab and office, and he felt like it was slowly killing him. Of course, according to his latest report, that might be moot.

He looked at his watch. It had a cartoon likeness of Albert Einstein, and the arms spun around and pointed out the time much like a Mickey Mouse watch. It hadn't run in years, but it was the last Father's Day present he ever received from his daughter, so the sentimental value was what kept it on his wrist. After he and his wife divorced, the relationship between him and his daughter deteriorated as well. She was now a senior in college, or maybe she had graduated, but he hadn't heard from her in a long time. Ironically, the job he missed so much, which might find him drilling for ice samples in the Arctic or releasing weather balloons in Ecuador, was perhaps the biggest factor in the divorce. Although he loved the work, he always felt that was what drove his wife and daughter away.

The door opened and a middle-aged woman in a dress suit appeared. "They're ready for you, Dr. McNair."

His bones creaked and moaned as he stood, raising his six-foot frame up from the low metal bench. He followed her inside and paid no attention to where she was motioning. He had been here before and knew where to go. He walked to the table in front of the raised platform where the five senators were poised and ready for their in-

48

terrogation and took a seat. The chair was padded but still hard on his slender haunches. His stomach was growling as if wondering why he hadn't sent any food its way all day.

The senators were all deep in their own thoughts, so Dr. McNair waited patiently. A shadow made him suddenly realize there was a presence behind him. He turned with a jolt. There stood a woman he guessed to be around fifty years old, tall, stern, with gray hair and haunting dark eyes.

"I believe you have my seat," she said.

Dr. McNair was taken aback. Although there were many seats in the room for public viewing of some issues handled by this committee, the public was never allowed for his visits, much less someone demanding his chair.

"Are you sure?" he asked politely.

The woman stood unflinching, so he got up and moved his briefcase to the end of the table and pulled up another chair. The woman sat and stared straight ahead.

"I'm Stephen McNair," he offered in truce.

She offered a slight smile. "I'm Glenda Eagle. Sorry about this. I shouldn't be long, but this is very important." She turned her head back toward the committee, then back to Dr. McNair. "What's your stuff about?"

Dr. McNair smiled. "Just the end of the world."

Glenda chuckled. "Well, I guess that might be considered important too."

He laughed at her semi-imitation of an apology.

"Okay, let's get started," Senator Elaine Biddle from Arkansas said. "Dr. McNair, if you don't mind, we promised Ms. Eagle ten minutes this morning and she flew all the way from Los Angeles."

"No, ma'am, I'm fine with that."

"Very well, Ms. Eagle, you have the floor," Senator Biddle said. "We haven't had time to go over your entire report, so why don't you sum it up."

Glenda stood and looked each senator in the eye before beginning. "The bottom line is, senators, we have to do something. There are over one-point-five million pit bulls put to death in this country every year. And those are conservative estimates. Plus, these numbers are only for those euthanized in the larger shelters. A lot of the smaller shelters don't keep records. And this doesn't include dogs killed in the fighting rings, or as bait dogs, or the strays that die of disease or starvation."

"Are these numbers real?"

Glenda looked at Senator Butler from Georgia. "I assure you they're real."

"I thought the shelters took in most of the dogs not wanted," Senator Biddle said. She glanced at the report in front of her. "Your organization . . . what's it called?"

"The Pit Stop," Glenda said.

"Yes," Senator Biddle said. "Aren't there a lot of shelters that take in pit bull dogs? Don't you have a large shelter?"

"There are, but nowhere near enough to save them all. I have a very large shelter. We can house almost a thousand dogs. But it still isn't enough."

"But you get government funding for this, no?" Senator Butler asked.

"No! I do not get a penny from the government," Glenda snapped. "All of our money comes from private donations."

"So what do you propose?" Senator Weingold from New York asked. "Should we outlaw pit bulls? I mean, haven't some towns done that already because of how vicious they are?"

Glenda's face turned red. "Senator, pit bulls aren't vicious, people are. There is no evidence to suggest that pit bulls are more violent or more aggressive than any other breed. In fact, pit bulls have never made the top-ten list of most reported dog bites."

"But haven't there been more fatalities with pits?" Senator Casey of Vermont chimed in.

"Yes, there have." Glenda was honest. "I'm not saying pit bulls are not stronger than other breeds. It's like asking which car is more dangerous: a minivan or a Ferrari. Neither is dangerous, but if you wreck a minivan going forty miles per hour and wreck a Ferrari going one hundred and fifty miles per hour, one is likely to have a more serious outcome."

The senators were all quiet. It wasn't clear they understood the analogy.

"Look," Glenda said, "the problem is not that people believe the horrible things that are said about pit bulls. The problem is that they don't believe them. People have come to know pit bulls as loving, gentle, loyal, protective members of their families. They are in big demand. As much damage as the fighters do, the more serious problem is the backyard breeders flooding the world with more pit bulls than we can find homes for. They have to be stopped."

"Wait," Senator Butler said. "Aren't there laws against that now?"

"Yes," Glenda scoffed. "It's a hundred-dollar fine. It's a joke. The breeders can get up to a thousand dollars for one puppy, so the fine means nothing."

"So give us your summation," Senator Biddle said.

"We have to come down hard on breeders. We have to also make it mandatory for anyone who gets a pit bull as a pet to have it spayed or neutered. We have to attack it from this end if we want to start making a dent in this one-point-five-million-a-year number."

Senator Weingold raised his hand. "Uh, excuse me, but if we make all breeding illegal, won't pit bulls become extinct?"

The other senators nodded in agreement as if wishing they had thought of that.

Glenda stared at the panel in disbelief. "No, senators. There are still millions of strays in this country. They estimate fifty thousand in Los Angeles County alone. There will still be more pit bulls bred every year than we can handle."

"There you go," Senator Butler said. "If someone wants a pit bull puppy, they can find a stray. Right?"

Glenda knew he was being sarcastic, but it made perfect sense

51

to her.

"Ms. Eagle," Senator Biddle said, "we will discuss this at length. I assure you it will not be taken lightly. There are a lot of dog lovers in Congress."

"Thank you for hearing me today." Glenda gathered her things and turned from the table.

Dr. McNair watched her stride out and envied her passion. Nothing had moved him like that in years.

"Thank you for coming, Doctor," Senator Biddle said.

Dr. McNair simply nodded.

"Well," the senator continued, "we've been looking over your last report and to tell you the truth, it's rather confusing."

Silence.

The senators all looked at one another. Senator Weingold from New York spoke up. "What she's trying to say is that it doesn't make sense. We don't understand what the report is saying."

"It is in English. Exactly what part don't you understand?"

Senator Biddle clarified. "This part about being 'irreversible.' This reads like it's a scare tactic to solicit more funding."

"You do not control my funding, senators, so why would I lie to you?"

Senator Butler from Georgia chimed in. "It's just that we've been hearing about this threat since the year 2000, or before, Doctor. It might have taken a while for everyone to acknowledge that global warming was real, but this is 2050. I think we've done a lot to reduce greenhouse gases in the last half century. There are more regulations on factories and at least thirty percent of the cars on the road today are electric. Plus, that new chemical is supposed to be eating away the greenhouse gases. Are you still trying to tell us we're not doing enough?"

Dr. McNair looked at the five-person panel. "It is true that GHR1101, which was introduced a decade ago, is working. It doesn't 'eat' greenhouse gases, but it slowly converts them into an ionized gas allowing it to filter through the stratosphere and into space. Current estimates put the accumulation of greenhouses gases in our atmosphere at ten percent of where they were ten years ago. So in theory, we should be going through a global cooling period, but that's not happening. As my report proves, we're headed for a disaster of biblical proportions. Sea levels have already risen over three inches in the last twenty years. If this trend continues, that will accelerate exponentially."

Senator Butler raised his hands beside him in a grand gesture and repeated his question. "Again, are we not doing enough? What should we be doing?"

Dr. McNair shook his head. "I'm telling you it doesn't matter what you do from this point forward; it cannot be stopped. The polar ice caps are melting at an alarming rate, not just from the surface air rising, but from the ocean water temps rising as well. If you could somehow stop all the carbon and methane emissions tomorrow, it would not stop what's happening."

"It's hard to believe, Doctor," Senator Weingold said, "that with today's technology, you're saying we can't make a difference."

"What technology are you referring to, Senator?" Dr. McNair looked around the room. "Would you try to drop ice cubes in the ocean or try to cool all the air in our atmosphere with air conditioners? There is no technology to stop this and certainly none to reverse it."

"What do you expect us to do with a report like this?" Senator Butler asked.

"I can only report the facts to you. What you decide to do is up to you." Dr. McNair began stuffing his papers back into his briefcase.

"How long, Doctor?"

Dr. McNair looked up at the female senator from North Dakota, the one who seldom got involved with the fray. "How long for what, Senator Malcolm?" he asked.

The senator cleared her throat. "How long before the melting ice changes the face of Earth forever? How long before the temperatures on Earth are unsuitable for humans?"

Dr. McNair continued to put away his papers without looking up. "Five years. Ten tops."

Before he could leave, Senator Biddle had one last question. "What would you suggest, Doctor?"

Dr. McNair paused only briefly before turning to leave. "I'd start building a really big boat." He walked out of the room and through the dimly lit corridor and back out into the sunshine. He paused to take a deep breath of air as if he had just crawled out of a deep cavern. He walked toward his car. Looking at the bright sunny sky, he debated whether to even return to work. Although it was only noon, he didn't relish going back to his office, but there was nothing for him at home either.

"Hey."

Dr. McNair turned to see who was behind him. "Oh, hey there. Mrs. Eagle, right?"

"It's *Miss* Eagle."

"Oh, in that case," Dr. McNair joked, holding out his hand, "I'm Stephen."

She shook his hand and smiled. "It was very nice of you to let me go first in there."

"Well, it wasn't really about being polite," Dr. McNair said with a smile. "You scare me."

Glenda laughed. "Let me make it up to you. My flight isn't for a couple of hours. Can I buy you lunch?"

"That's the best offer I've had in a long time."

"Great," Glenda said. "While we eat you can tell me when the world is going to end."

"*Pfftttt.*" Dr. McNair smirked. "Boring. I want to hear more about your pit bulls."

"How can this be the right way?" Darren glanced over to his boss, Dr. De Luca, and then back to the SETI director, Dr. Natalie Zimmerman.

"We can't go to the president or secretary of defense without evidence," Dr. Zimmerman snapped. "And we will not be creating a worldwide panic when we don't know what this signal is. It could be directed at Earth accidentally."

Natalie Zimmerman wore a suit as well as any man, but she was much more masculine than most men were. Her blonde hair was spiked upward with enough mousse to make concrete out of Jell-O. Not a trace of makeup or jewelry to be seen. She was barely over five feet tall and as wide as she was tall. When she walked, her shoulders stayed perfectly perpendicular to the direction she was going, and the swift short movements of her legs made her mimic the movements of a tank or bulldozer. In fact, "Dozer" was the name everyone called her when she wasn't around.

Dr. De Luca stood with Darren. "Director, the signal is real and not of this world. And it's getting closer. I agree with Darren on this. The worst-case scenario is that we go public, inform the White House, and nothing ever comes from it and we look stupid. Or the other worst-case scenario could be we keep it a secret, and something does come from it and we look incompetent."

Dr. Zimmerman wouldn't budge. "It's not a matter of appearances. As long as I'm in charge, we follow protocol." She looked at Darren. "I want you to head up this investigation from the Washington office. You'll have everything you need and get to put together your team. It's still your baby. Don't make me regret that decision."

"Thank you." Darren was glad to be in charge of that at least. "When do I leave?"

"About noon tomorrow."

Darren stayed up late that night going over tons of data. Although the signal had now been verified by every SETI lab in the world, they still knew nothing about the signal, like what it was saying or why it was directed at the oceans.

His two bosses slept in a rented RV while he and Roscoe had the lab to themselves.

"What do you think?" Darren asked of Roscoe. "You're the real one who discovered the signal. It should be called the 'Roscoe Signal' instead of the 'Mitchell Signal.'"

Roscoe yawned. Apparently he had no opinion at all.

Darren finally got to bed around 2:00 a.m. but couldn't sleep. This was, after all, the biggest thing that had ever happened to him, perhaps to anyone. He finally got up at six and continued packing his stuff.

An hour later, Dr. De Luca and Dr. Zimmerman returned and helped him finish getting ready before they said their good-byes.

After they left the lab, Darren took a look around. He hadn't been here long enough to grow attached to anything and was glad to be leaving, but one thing had happened that he couldn't forget. He decided to make one last trip into town, this time in the truck.

As he drove around with Roscoe in the passenger side, he searched for the Chevrolet Impala, hoping to find Francisco before running into the other bunch. Finally he saw him standing beside his car on what would most likely be called the main street in town. He was talking to a beautiful Mexican girl. As the girl walked away, Darren pulled the truck up beside him.

"Hey, Roscoe." Francisco walked around to the passenger side and started petting Roscoe through the window. "Sorry, man, I didn't catch your name."

"I'm Darren."

"So what's going on out there?" Francisco asked while still playing with Roscoe. "I saw the big fancy travel lodge. You guys discover life on Mars finally?"

"No, just a new star."

Francisco looked skeptical. "That fancy RV showed up for a star." He shook his head in disbelief.

Darren didn't try to sell the lie. "I'm leaving this morning, so I wanted to come find you and thank you again and give you this." He held out a small object.

Francisco looked puzzled but took the object and looked at it. It appeared to be a stone in the shape of a tooth on a leather string. "What is it ?"

"It's a fossilized tooth from a prehistoric canine. I found it in Nevada."

Francisco smiled. "That's very neat. You didn't have to do that, but I appreciate it. So you're leaving, huh? Are you coming back?"

"I don't think so. They're sending me to the office in Washington, DC."

"Of course," Francisco said and chuckled, "to study this new star."

Darren smiled.

Francisco rubbed Roscoe on both sides of his head. "You take care of this boy, you hear?"

"I will," Darren said.

"I was talking to Roscoe."

Darren smiled and stuck out his hand. "Take care."

"You too, amigo." Francisco shook his hand.

As Francisco watched Darren drive away, he continued to his destination. He walked up to a small house and knocked on the door. A woman opened the door and smiled.

"*Hola*, Mama."

Rosita Escamilla opened her arms and hugged her son. "I haven't seen you in weeks. How can that be in a town this small? Why don't you come see your mama more?"

"I've been busy working."

"Work, huh?" His mama scoffed.

"*Sí*, work." Francisco took out a small stack of cash and handed it to his mama.

"Where did you get this?"

Francisco shook his head. "I told you—work. Now please get a refill on your medication. Please."

"Hey, Frankie."

Francisco smiled as his pretty ten-year-old sister ran into his arms, her long black hair shining in the light. He caught her in his arms and lifted her as high as he could. "How's my Chiquita?"

"Call me Maria. I'm not that small anymore," she said.

He stood her up and held his hand above her head. "*Sí*, you're growing like a weed, Chiquita."

"Can you stay for lunch?" Ms. Escamilla asked.

"Absolutely."

Maria giggled. "Tell me a story, Frankie."

His mama went to finish cooking as he sat on the couch with his sister. He took out his new gift from Darren and showed it to her.

"Do you see this?"

Maria's eyes were wide open as she ran her little fingers over the fossilized tooth. "What is it?"

"I was walking through the desert last week," Francisco began, "when this huge dog started to chase me. It was like a dinosaur it was so big. It chased me and tried to eat me." He grabbed Maria under each arm and tickled until she begged for mercy.

"What did you do?" she asked when she finished laughing.

"What do you think I did? I ran as fast as I could. Then it chased me up a tree and stayed at the bottom waiting for me to come down. I stayed high in the tree until night came. I couldn't wait to get away so I could tell everyone about the ferocious beast. But I knew they wouldn't believe me, so when the monster dog was sleeping, I climbed back down the tree, took my knife, and cut out his tooth."

"What did he do?" Maria asked.

"He yelled, 'Ouch!' and tried harder to get me."

Francisco continued to spin a yarn of immense proportions, much to the delight of his little sister. Finally their mama called them to eat. They each went to the bathroom to wash their hands and joined their mama at the small Formica kitchen table.

"Will you say grace, Francisco?" his mama asked.

Francisco nodded. He asked the blessing, and they dined on homemade tamales and drank real lemonade until they were full. Afterward, they sat around the table and chatted for a long time. It was like they were a family again all under the same roof. They had a good time being together, until Francisco's cell phone rang. His mama watched suspiciously.

"*Hola?* Yes, I can come by. I'll be there soon."

"More *work?*" his mama asked sarcastically.

Francisco smiled. "No, Mama. That was Ms. Rhonda at the shelter. They have a new dog and need some help."

His mama dropped her head. "I'm sorry. Go help them. You know I worry about you."

"And I worry about you. Please get a refill. Okay?"

Maria came up and hugged him around the waist.

"And get Chiquita here some vitamins so she can finally grow."

His mama nodded as he left the house.

Thirty minutes later, Francisco pulled his car up to the dog shelter outside of town. It was an old vegetable processing plant from years ago, but now it was just a large, rickety old shed that Ms. Rhonda, an old American woman, had converted into the only shelter for many towns around. No one knew where Ms. Rhonda came from. She just showed up one day about eight years ago with the deed to this property and a carload of pit bulls.

It was hard to tell her age, because her skin was wrinkled more than normal due to hard work and the desert sun. She always wore a huge sombrero to protect herself from the harsh rays. She seemed to wear the same faded jeans and flannel shirt with the sleeves cut off every day. She was very short and thin and appeared very frail, but everyone knew better. Many times the citizens of El Triunfo had seen her carrying fifty-pound bags of dog food and more than once had witnessed her carrying a full-grown pit bull over her shoulders to bring to the doctor in town.

She had paid someone to drag an old pop-up camper out here and it now represented her living quarters, although she spent much more time under the shed with the dogs. Word got around fast, and for many towns around if people found a stray or couldn't take care of their own pit bulls, they brought them to Ms. Rhonda.

Ms. Rhonda and her two volunteers met him at his car.

"Where is he?" Francisco asked.

"He's back here," Ms. Rhonda said and led him inside.

They passed about fifteen stalls with unwanted or stray pits until they got to the last stall. Inside was a very large, very dirty, very scarred, and very angry pit bull. He was a unique color, white with feathered spots and a large circle that wrapped around his back like a saddle, which was a brindled brown with black stripes. Half of his huge head was the same brindled color. The rest was white with the little speckles. He wore a muzzle to keep him from biting anyone. He lunged at the gate as Francisco walked up.

"We think he was a fighting dog," Ms. Rhonda said.

"Doubtful. He's still alive. I'm betting he wouldn't fight so they used him for training." Francisco shook his head and wondered how anyone could do that to such a beautiful animal. "Come here," he said.

The dog lunged again and Francisco caught his collar. He held him tight and worked the buckle on the side of the muzzle and slid it off. He let go of the collar, and the dog seized the opportunity of no longer having the muzzle to growl and bite at Francisco.

Francisco looked at Ms. Rhonda and the two young Mexican boys who helped her out.

"Oh right. Let's go, boys, and leave Francisco and Beast alone." Ms. Rhonda knew how he liked to work, so they excused themselves. Francisco preferred no distractions when trying to gain a dog's trust.

"Beast, huh?" Francisco asked. "That sounds like a good name for you."

The dog ran circles inside the little stall, knocking over his food and water dish. Francisco waited for several minutes, letting the dog get used to his presence, then picked up the gallon jug outside the stall and opened the gate. He walked in as if he owned the stall and closed the gate behind him. The dog took a defensive stance and bared his teeth. Francisco ignored him and walked right past and turned the water bowl upright and filled it.

The dog kept his head turned toward Francisco wherever he went. Francisco continued to ignore the dog and acted as if this were his home. After he filled the dish with water, he simply sat down on the ground with his back up against the back wall of the stall and did nothing. He didn't address the dog or say anything at all. In fact, after about fifteen minutes, he started to doze off.

Francisco woke up from a short nap. The dog was lying down now, still watching Francisco and breathing hard, but no longer growling. "See, I'm not going to hurt you. We'll just hang out until you trust me."

Francisco took another nap. When he woke the next time, the dog was napping only a few feet from him. He smiled and drifted off again.

The next time he woke, the dog was still sleeping but with his head in Francisco's lap. He reached down and began rubbing the dog's head, then his back, then his belly. The dog rolled onto its back to give him a better angle.

When Francisco rose, the dog jumped up and growled.

"It's okay, big boy," Francisco said in a reassuring tone. "I'll be right back."

He walked back to the front of the building and found Ms. Rhonda.

"How goes it?" she asked.

Francisco gave a thumbs-up. "Just came to get some treats."

Ms. Rhonda gladly gave him some. "How do you do it?"

He shrugged. "Dogs have always liked me. Maybe I'm part dog."

They both laughed as Francisco turned to go back. He opened the gate and the large pit bull growled again. Once more, Francisco ignored him and took his seat, but this time he held up a doggie treat. The former fighter or bait dog cocked his head as if trying to figure this guy out. He inched closer and sniffed the treat. Finally he gingerly took the treat in his teeth and walked away to devour it.

Francisco held up another. The dog was a little quicker this time and didn't walk away to eat it.

The day progressed until the sun was hanging lazily in the western sky. Ms. Rhonda figured enough time had passed, and she hadn't heard any barking or growling, so she slowly walked to the back stall. "Oh my goodness," she said as she saw Francisco lying on the ground wrestling with the big pit bull. They were having a good time together.

Francisco looked up at Ms. Rhonda and smiled. "He's just a big old teddy bear. Aren't you, Gentle Beast?"

"Gentle Beast, huh?" Ms. Rhonda asked.

"Yeah, I think it fits him better."

The dog leaped up on the gate when Ms. Rhonda walked up, but with no aggression. She ran her hands along each side of his head and behind his ears. He was enjoying the attention.

Francisco walked out of the stall. "He'll be okay now."

"I don't know how you do this, but thanks again." Ms. Rhonda stuck her hand in her pocket. "I don't have much, but please let me pay you this time."

He held up his hand. "I thought you were going to offer me a doggie treat."

They both laughed.

"Seriously, I'm glad to do it. Call me whenever you need me."

Gentle Beast started to whine as Francisco walked away.

"Don't worry, boy, I'll be back to see you." He walked to his car, waved, and drove away.

"I can't believe you always get up so early," Dr. McNair said into the telephone.

"I don't have much choice," Glenda Eagle said on the other end of the line. "Not when you have this many dogs to take care of."

"I can imagine. I just wanted to give you a call before going to work. I have to leave for my office in a few minutes."

"Do you still enjoy it?" Glenda asked.

"No, I hate it," Dr. McNair answered. "This office job is slowly killing me. I stare out of the window most of the time wishing I were still in the field. I am seriously considering retiring."

"I think you just need a vacation. You know, somewhere nice and warm."

Dr. McNair laughed. "Tell me a place this day and age where it's not warm. That's my job, trying to find where the planet is not warm anymore, or at least discover why it's not ever going to be cool again. And I apparently suck at it."

Glenda laughed. "Maybe you're spending too much time looking out the window."

"Maybe. Maybe you're right about that vacation."

Glenda went for the kill. "How about California? I'm not sure if you're aware of this or not, but that is actually a family favorite of states to visit during vacation. Heck, some people come every year."

"Really?" Dr. McNair said. "I did not know that. You guys have some cool stuff out that way?"

"We've got some stuff. I know this great place where you can bury yourself up to your eyeballs in doggie kisses and forget about everything else."

"Sounds tempting," Dr. McNair said. "But I have to be honest with you; I've never owned a dog."

"Never?" Glenda said, shocked. "How is that possible? Not even as a little boy?"

"Nope. My dad wasn't a big animal lover of any kind. When I got married, my wife and I talked about it a few times, but then she got pregnant and after the baby came along, we just didn't think about it anymore."

"That's the saddest thing I've ever heard," Glenda said. "You definitely need to come spend some time here. You'll leave here wanting to take a couple of these guys home with you."

Dr. McNair let that paint a picture in his mind. "I'm not sure how good a dog owner I would be. I can hardly take care of myself."

"Well, for one thing," Glenda said, "you would stop referring to yourself as an 'owner' and start referring to yourself as a 'parent.' Dogs are members of the family, not possessions."

"See, I still have a lot to learn."

"Yes, you do," Glenda said. "It's a good thing we met, huh? Who better to guide you through this process?"

Dr. McNair smiled. He certainly admired her passion for dogs, especially pit bulls. "I wish we could talk vacations and dogs all day, but I have to go. I'll give you a call this evening."

"Okay, bye."

Dr. McNair hung up the phone, got dressed for work, and walked out to his car. Even this early he cranked the air conditioning up to high for the daily commute. Once he got to his block, he navigated his car around the front of the US Climatology building and noticed the protestors were back. He couldn't understand why they picketed his building. They were only scientists reporting the events of global warming, not creating it.

After turning down beside the building and parking in the employee parking lot, he got out of the car with a bag carrying his fast-food breakfast. He was notorious for eating junk food on demand since he rarely had the time to get away from work or the inclination to cook at home.

As he neared the coded front entrance, a young Asian woman with a briefcase was waiting by the door. She was short, athletic, and wearing a shapely pantsuit. Her short black hair came to her shoulders and reflected the morning sun.

"Are you Dr. Stephen McNair?" she asked.

Dr. McNair looked longingly at the bag in his hand carrying his first meal of the day. He nodded.

She stuck out her hand. "I'm Sally Xie. I've been leaving you messages for several days now."

"Salacy?"

She grinned. "No. First name: Sally. Last name: Xie. You can call me Sally. I'm a marine—"

As she stopped and stared past him, Dr. McNair turned to see what had distracted her. A large man with a picket sign was strolling straight toward them. He was about six feet five, with long brown hair that came down in front of him well past his shoulders, and a matching beard. He wore baggy clothes but still presented a formidable appearance. His shoulders were broad and arms thick. He looked like Jesus on steroids.

"Dr. McNair," he shouted as he walked up, "do you really think you're fooling anyone with your government cover-up? We know what's really happening. The people have a right to know the truth. Don't you agree?"

Dr. McNair looked up at the sign, which read, "THEY are real." Looking at some of the other signs, he noticed the general theme for all of them was of aliens and terraforming. He stuck out his hand to the big guy. "I'm all for the truth. Call me Stephen. I'm not sure who *they* are, but if you're referring to aliens from another planet, I have no data at all on that, so there is no cover-up. As a scientist, however, I won't rule out anything. If you have a few minutes, I'd love to hear what evidence you have."

It was a brilliant move. It defused the big man's steam. He was actually quite shocked but shook Dr. McNair's hand. "Yeah, sure. My name is Thomas Freeman. Thank you, Stephen. I have lots of evidence from hundreds of hours of research and it speaks for itself. Perhaps you've read my books."

"I don't believe so." Dr. McNair looked back to Sally. "Oh, this is Sally. She's a marine."

Thomas snapped to attention and presented a real-life salute. "*Semper fi*, ma'am. I was class of 2039 Parris Island myself."

Sally shook her head. "No, I'm a marine *biologist*." She turned back to Dr. McNair. "Sir, I need to speak to you about a matter of grave concern."

"And my concern is not grave?" Thomas asked.

"Regardless," Sally said. "I believe I was first here."

Dr. McNair glanced at both of them. They looked like they would be good distractions from actually going to work. "I'll see you both, but pardon me while I eat."

He led them to his office and sat behind the desk as they seated themselves in the two padded wingback chairs in front of the desk. "Okay, since we're on a first name basis, Thomas, tell me what you know." He took out the first biscuit and sank his teeth into it.

Thomas seemed to like being called on first. "Okay. First, are you familiar with Dr. Niklasson's research?"

Dr. McNair nodded and continued to chew.

"What is that?" Sally asked.

Dr. McNair wiped the corners of his mouth. "A Swedish scientist who developed a scale model of Earth, which can simulate the atmosphere, weather, climate, etcetera. His latest report stipulates that in all of his trials, neither greenhouse gases nor any planetary events could produce the kind of global warming we are experiencing."

Thomas nodded. "Exactly. So if we are not doing it ourselves, who is? Scientists have also discovered pyramids on the ocean floor, about a dozen or so, and carbon dating puts them over a million years old, way before man could have made them."

Dr. McNair bit into his second biscuit. "I don't see the connection," he said while chewing.

"Once again," Thomas said, "if humans didn't build them, who did?" The office was quite silent so he continued. "See, we've always believed that aliens were heating the planet from the outside. But, what if they are using the Earth's own resources? What if they have devices on the ocean floor that have pipes going down into the earth, down where it's a lot hotter near the core? It would release the heat up through the seawater and heat the atmosphere."

"Wow," Sally said. "I really thought you were just a nutcase."

Dr. McNair laughed as he dusted crumbs off his shirt. "So did I."

Thomas also laughed. "Well, I might be a little." Then he looked at Sally. "Perhaps you've read my books."

"May I say something?" Sally asked, ignoring the last comment.

Thomas nodded.

"It's amazing you say that because it coincides with what I was going to mention, at least one of the things." Sally opened her briefcase and produced a stack of papers. "I wondered also if greenhouse gases were to blame, or any other man-made scenario. If we were indeed heating the air, wouldn't it heat the water evenly?"

"Not necessarily," Dr. McNair said. "There would be several variables. For instance, the depth and speed of the water would be huge factors."

"Exactly," she said and slid a large map across the desk. "I got this from the National Oceanographic Data Center. It shows the areas where the ocean temps have become the most elevated. You'll notice that they all are aligned with the ocean currents like the Gulf Stream. These are the areas of the deepest and fastest-moving waters."

Dr. McNair put on his reading glasses, picked up the map, and stared at it.

Sally continued. "It just seems those would be the areas least affected. And since warmer air around the entire planet would wreak havoc on shallow and stagnant water more, why isn't it raising the temps for all the lakes in the world?"

"Those are good questions," Thomas said.

"It's not just the temps either."

Dr. McNair looked up over his reading glasses. "Yes?"

Sally slid another paper across the desk. "We tag and track as many animals as we can. This shows the migration of a young humpback named Walter—"

Dr. McNair laughed. As Sally stared at him, he apologized. "Sorry. I just think it's funny that you give human names to fish."

"Mammals," she corrected. "And that hardly seems appropriate coming from a man who gives human names to storms."

Thomas laughed so hard he almost fell out of the chair. "She got you there."

"Touché," Dr. McNair said. "Please continue."

Sally ran a finger along the dotted line on the paper. "This young whale, and several others we monitor, has begun migrating along the currents. These are highly unusual patterns. And it's not just that."

Thomas and Dr. McNair were paying close attention.

"In the last few years, there have been many reports of ocean mammals acting very odd, even attacking divers. This is not their usual behavior."

"Why?" Thomas asked.

She shrugged. "We just don't know."

"They are mammals as you say," Dr. McNair said, "so why would any mammal do this? Why would land mammals do this?"

Sally looked at Thomas as if afraid to answer. "Well, there's only one reason we know of. This is how mammals act if there's a very dangerous or foreign predator around. Some dogs have attacked their own masters when bears or other large predators come within their vicinity."

Thomas sat back and smiled. "I knew it; it's aliens."

Dr. McNair looked at Sally. "Is that what you're saying?"

"No. I never even considered that."

"But now?" Thomas asked.

"No, not even now," Sally snapped.

"Boy, you sure are pretty when you're angry," Thomas said with a grin. "Do you have a boyfriend?"

"Can we please stick to the matter at hand?" Sally asked.

Thomas continued to push it. "We can make this the matter at hand."

"I don't have a boyfriend," Sally said, giving in. "I don't need or want one either. I don't have time. And even if I did, it wouldn't be a wacko who believes in the bogeyman."

"I like a feisty woman," Thomas said.

"Dr. McNair, please, a little help here."

Dr. McNair had been taking the opportunity of them sparring over boyfriend-girlfriend stuff to finish his meal. He threw the empty bag in the trash and looked again at the map. "You make some fine points, Ms. Xie. If global warming was being caused by the atmosphere getting hotter, it should heat the water according to certain variables. As for whales traveling the Gulf Stream, I'm afraid that's out of my territory."

"Maybe they're just lost," Thomas offered. "I mean, whales aren't very bright, are they?"

Sally almost went off on him until she noticed the devious smile and realized he was baiting her.

"Wait," Dr. McNair said, holding the first map, the one with the dotted current lines and measurements of water temps. "What's this line? Is it an error on the photo?"

Sally and Thomas leaned in. Not far off the westernmost point of North Africa was a very faint shadow.

"I'm sure that's just a printing error," Sally said.

Dr. McNair started punching the keys on his computer. "Let's get a current satellite view." He played with the mouse and keyboard until he got what he wanted. He looked up at them both. "You're not going to believe this."

Both of them jumped out of their seats and walked around

behind him, one on each side. They stared at the large computer screen in awe. There was the same faint line.

"It's probably just a reef," Sally said.

"Visible from space?" Dr. McNair asked.

"Maybe a whale," Thomas said.

Dr. McNair put two fingers on the lines at the bottom of the map that marked the length in miles, then on the mystery line. "Yep, could be a whale, if whales grow to a hundred miles long."

Thomas leaned a little closer. "It looks like the outline of a spaceship to me."

Sally scoffed.

Dr. McNair smiled as he realized the opportunity for an expedition had finally presented itself. "Whatever it is, we need to find out. Who's up for a field trip?"

Sally nodded.

"You want me to go too?" Thomas asked.

Dr. McNair leaned back in his chair and stared up at him. "You're the only alien expert we have."

Thomas smiled. "I'm in. Who's buying?"

"The Climatology Department can pick up the bill, even though this is more your area, Ms. Xie," Dr. McNair said.

"Why don't we have the coast guard or someone go by there?" Sally asked.

"Not a chance," Dr. McNair said. "Okay, Thomas and I will go without you."

"No, no," Sally said. "I'm in."

"Great," Thomas said. Then he looked at Sally. "But just remember, this is a professional investigation. No funny stuff."

"Are you sure you want to take the class clown?" Sally asked.

"Of course, I'm sure," Dr. McNair said.

"Thank you, Stephen." Thomas sat back with his chest sticking out in pride.

"Because if we really find aliens," Dr. McNair said, "I want someone expendable to sacrifice so we can get away."

9

"Why didn't we get a launch confirmation?" General Nickerson huffed as he leaned over the airman's shoulder, his frustration actually seeming to raise the temperature in the tomb of electronic devices, the control room at NORAD. He was a large man, over 240 pounds, and stood over six feet tall. He was a daunting figure by all standards, especially to those of lower rank, but this situation was making him even more intimidating.

Airman Rodriguez squirmed a little uncomfortably in his seat. He didn't answer. He kept staring at the screen as if the answer might appear, but the screen took the Fifth Amendment.

Every controller in the room sat up straighter while they stared at their own screens as if hoping to aid the airman's lack of an answer. But it turned into a library as you could even hear the general's breathing.

"What's the target?" the general asked.

The airman punched a few buttons, and the left big screen in the front of the huge room filled with the world map outline. "Central America, sir. It looks like the inbound will hit Panama. There are six total."

The general stared at the big screen and rubbed his chin. His large frame breathed heavily, making the three stars on each shoulder rise and fall. Perspiration began to form on his bald head. "Panama? Who would want to bomb Panama?"

"Maybe they're going after the canal," another airman said.

"Good God . . . why?" The general stared at the airman to let him know it wasn't a rhetorical question. "And who? If they wanted to take out the canal, surely there are easier ways. Heck, just fill a ship with explosives. There are a million ways to accomplish that without using long-range missiles."

"Sir," Airman Rodriguez said, "I don't believe they are missiles. They're moving too fast and they are much larger than any weapon I'm aware of."

"Do we have a visual?" the general asked.

One of the civilian operatives spoke up. "General, we have an AWACS in the gulf. They can get us a long-distance shot."

"Do it." The general walked toward the front and waited. After several seconds he looked back at the operative, who appeared to be getting a little nervous.

"It's coming through now, sir."

The second screen filled with a cloudless blue void as the general adjusted his glasses and squinted. There they were: six tiny black lines that seemed to be stationary. With no reference other than the sky, they looked like tiny scratches on the screen.

"You're right," the general said. "Those aren't missiles. So what the heck are they?"

The airman with the canal idea spoke again. "Maybe they're meteorites."

The general turned and looked at the young soldier as if he were impaired in some way. "Meteorites? Falling in formation? And what, they have been hurtling at Earth visible to our radar for years and we just missed them? Is that what you're telling me, son? And if they're meteorites, where's the fire? Why aren't they burning up in our atmosphere?"

No one had an answer.

"But it's certain they didn't fly here through the air," the general said. "So that leaves only one place they could have come from—space. Contact NASA and see what they know."

Everyone worked feverishly trying to provide some answers, or at least make it look as if they were searching. NORAD had been established in 1958 as a joint effort between the governments of the United States and Canada with the simple mission of providing warning and defense from surprise attacks over North America. And even though the objects were not heading for North America, there was no guarantee that others would not appear over the sovereign area. In all that time, never had there been an attack to warn people about—not once.

A man in a black suit and tie entered the room. "General, the president and vice president have been moved to PEOC. All of the information you're tracking here will be sent to that new location."

The general looked confused. "The Presidential Emergency Operations Center? I thought that was for nuclear attack. Do you guys at NSA know what's going on?"

"No, sir. We do not."

"Tell me what you do know," the general said.

The man looked around the room as if wondering if he should divulge classified information. He leaned in and whispered. "Sir, we've heard from Russia and the United Kingdom. They're as stumped as we are. But they verified that no missiles have left Europe, Asia, or the Middle East."

The general didn't respond. He already knew that it wasn't missiles. He didn't want to know what the incoming objects were not; he wanted to know what they were.

The man in the black suit excused himself and left the room.

Another person spoke up. "General, NASA says all space is clear above the objects. In fact, they say there is nothing visible anywhere in space other than the space station and known satellites."

The general started pacing back and forth. He didn't know what was happening or what they should be doing. He looked around the room at the people stationed in front of monitors and could tell by their demeanor that they were as lost as he. He wondered if it was only a test but doubted the government would go to such measures. "How long before impact?" the general asked.

"Four minutes, thirty seconds, sir," Airman Rodriguez answered.

"That's fast. Get me a satellite visual," General Nickerson commanded.

The third screen illuminated with a live aerial view of Panama. Everyone stopped what they were doing to stare at the large monitor.

The general walked even closer to the screen. "Zoom in."

The image popped forward several times until only the northern part of Panama occupied the entire screen. Slowly it began to focus on the new view. With each blink of the image, it became more and more clear. As the pixels reached their limit, the scene was quite visible. Above the coastlines of Panama, starting just north of the canal, were six circles, brown dots along the coastline, three on each side of the country. But what were they?

The general turned away from the screen. "Get me the president."

Several minutes passed as they got President Patterson on the phone, whereupon the general explained the situation.

"But you're sure they're not missiles, General?" the president asked.

"We don't believe so, Mr. President. But we have no clue what they are. I wanted to ask if you could contact the president of Panama and find out what they know, and see if they can get us some pictures from the ground."

"I'll see what I can do."

After the general hung up the phone, he looked again to Airman Rodriguez. "Show me where all our ships and subs are."

The airman punched a few buttons and the screen displayed red images for subs and blue images for ships on the outline map.

The general just stood there and scratched his chin.

"Sir, we have impact," said Airman Rodriguez.

"Can the AWACS get closer to try to get us a better image?" the general asked.

Before anyone could answer, another person in the room spoke. "General, we have images from ground level. A Panama news crew is at the top middle projectile."

Everyone stared at the fourth screen. As the video came into focus, the crew could see the objects were in fact huge columns, which had literally been driven into the sands just off the coastlines of Panama in the Pacific Ocean and Caribbean Sea, like tent spikes might be driven into the ground. They were approximately twenty feet in diameter and towered high above the water into the sky. The sheer mass was an awesome sight to behold. They seemed to be made of stone, or possibly an unknown metal. The designs were intricate with carvings, or perhaps a type of writing, and the top of each column had a huge smooth white area at least twenty feet in length itself.

The general walked forward and leaned against the guardrail separating the monitors from the front wall, his hands clenched like vices as the blood rushed from the knuckles. He looked down and breathed heavily, thinking about the day he had been assigned to this post. He had been angry, had felt betrayed even, thinking this was the army's way of telling him he was no longer of use. He would spend the remainder of a long career staring at computer screens and getting excited whenever a weather balloon set off an alarm and was yet to be identified. After all, nothing ever happened here. Nothing ever had. Many times he had considered it might be time to hang up his stars.

"Sir?" a soldier sitting in front of another monitor said, bringing the general back to reality.

When the general looked around, the soldier simply nodded to the screen. The general turned and noticed the news crew had waded out into the water about waist deep and were using a small hammer to try to take a sample of the object. The general laughed. "Sure, why not? This thing just came from space, sped through our atmosphere without so much as losing any mass, so why not go out there and whack on it?"

"We're getting a feed from another news crew," Airman Rodriguez said. "General, you need to see this."

The general reacted by turning to the fifth and last screen to the right. The new footage came into view. "What am I looking at here? They're filming the sky?"

"Look at the distortion, sir."

The general backed up to see if it would help him make out the image. He saw it. A large round area of the sky was blurry, as if he were looking through an old window. "What is that?" the general asked. He turned to look at the airman.

"I don't know, sir, but it's getting larger."

The general looked again. It was clear the area of the distortion was growing in size as the diameter seemed to be continually expanding. Then it dawned on him. "No, son, not larger; it's getting lower."

The circular area in the sky descended until it hit the forest, breaking and flattening trees as it met the earth in an area approximately the size of a football field. The camera crew moved in. It looked as if you could see through it, albeit not clearly.

"What is that?" the general asked again, out loud to anyone.

The video feed started breaking up, and it was clear that the people of the news crew were seriously scared. Some turned and fled. Others seemed frozen, unable to move. One walked close enough to throw a rock at the semitransparent area. It flew through the air and suddenly bounced off an invisible object. After seeing that, a few others turned to flee.

"What in God's name?" the general asked. He turned to face the rest of the crew in NORAD. "We need answers, people. Keep searching the skies for any other projectiles anywhere else in the world. Okay, since we don't have facts, I want your thoughts. What are the columns for and why did they precede this . . . this . . . other thing?"

"Maybe they're there to mark the landing zone," a female airman said.

"Very good," the general said with a nod. "So we're already assuming it's a spaceship? Is that the general consensus in this room?"

Silence.

"What else? Anyone?" The general slowly turned to take in the entire populated area of the room.

"Maybe they're there to protect it," Airman Rodriguez offered.

"Son, you should be an officer. I'm going to recommend you for OCS." The general paced back and forth. "If your theory is correct, Airman, we have some serious problems. For one thing, how will they protect the ship and why? Are they weapons? And if they're already prepared for us to possibly attack them, then what are their intentions?"

"Sir, it's the president."

General Nickerson walked over and took the phone from a young airman. "Nickerson here."

"What have we learned, General?" the president asked.

"Not much I'm afraid, sir. Have you seen the footage of the object?"

"Yes, we're looking at it now," came the president's reply. "What do you make of it, General?"

"We actually believe it's a ship, sir, as crazy as that seems." The general thought about how farfetched his own words were sounding right now. "We think the larger columns that fell before it are to either mark the landing area or are perhaps here to protect the ship."

"Protect it?" the president asked. "Protect it from what?"

"From us, sir."

There were several seconds of silence before the president spoke again. "What do you suggest, General?"

"I don't think we should hesitate, sir. Let's take it out before it has a chance to take us out."

"What if their intentions are benign?" the president asked.

"Sir, if they were here on a friendly visit, I think they could have made that clear." The general stared at the fuzzy screen showing the distorted area. "I mean, they snuck up on our planet; they sent six huge projectiles at us without so much as a warning, and they have actually landed in a stealth-capable ship, sir. If you put two and two together, it's always going to be four. I say we get the country of Panama to give an evacuation order and we nuke the hell out of them . . . sir."

Another several seconds passed before President Patterson spoke. "No, we cannot attack without provocation."

The general shook his head. "Then at least let us position most of our ships and subs just off the shore there."

"No," the president said. "That could be construed as confrontational. I don't want to give them any reason to believe our actions are hostile. We will keep monitoring them until we know more. Good-bye, General."

The general mumbled under his breath as he hung up the phone.

Hours passed with no changes. A garrison of Panamanian soldiers was deployed to set up camp around the unknown object. There were a few skirmishes between the soldiers and the news crews, but they allowed them to stay on scene.

Lunch was brought into the NORAD command center and the general sat down to eat.

"Something's happening!" someone yelled.

The general dropped his fork and rushed to the railing to stare at the screen. "Holy Mary Mother of God," the general whispered.

What happened next ignited his spine with tingles. Everyone in the room gasped as the screen flashed and went blank.

The general turned away from the screen and began barking orders. "Send this to the president. Contact the Panama government and see if we can avert this video from hitting the Internet. Ground or reroute all flights going through this area. Let's see if we can close the canal and pull our ships out until we know what's going on. And someone get me SETI on the phone."

10

"This city has really grown," Dr. McNair said, looking out the window.

"The entire continent from what I've heard," Sally added.

After leaving the hotel, Sally maneuvered the rental car through the streets of Nouakchott. It was a blistering hot day, worse even than the abnormally hot days that had become the norm in the United States. She wore khaki pants and shirt with hiking boots. Dr. McNair was dressed similarly, sitting in the passenger side. Thomas sat in the back wearing a tank top, shorts, and sandals, looking more like a guy on vacation, his muscular body on full display.

Thomas pointed out the back window. "Hey, there's a casino. Let's hit the blackjack tables when we get back."

"I prefer to hold on to my money," Sally said. "I can think of many more things I could use it for besides giving it all away."

Thomas grinned toward her eyes in the rearview mirror. "I understand. You must know I have a birthday coming up."

"You are incorrigible," Sally shot back. "And roll up your window; the air conditioning is on."

"Are you sure?" Thomas held his arm out the window to direct the flow of air to his face. "I can't tell it's on."

"Me either," Dr. McNair said and rolled down his window.

Sally gave in and did the same. She navigated the car through the busy streets and followed the signs toward the public beach area and parked. As she opened the trunk, Thomas volunteered to carry her scuba gear.

They walked past the few people swimming and playing on

the beach. The beach area was stunning, with beautiful light-brown sand and crystal clear blue-green waters. But the heat was relentless, so very few were taking advantage of such an awesome beach, and most stayed under huge umbrellas. From the light color of their skin, they all appeared to be tourists.

"How do people live in this heat day to day?" Sally asked, looking back toward the city.

"I guess it's just what you get used to," Dr. McNair said, wiping the perspiration from his forehead.

Thomas tugged at the front of his tank top. "I can work on my tan while I'm here."

"Good idea," Sally said. "You're only two shades darker than the natives as it is." Her eyes glanced at Thomas's chest. She quickly looked away, but it did not go unnoticed.

"That's okay, honey bunny," Thomas said with a twinkle in his eyes. "You can stare all you like. I don't charge for that."

"That's good," Dr. McNair said. "I was getting ready to stick a dollar in your shorts."

They all laughed.

At the end of the beach was a wooden dock that ran parallel to the beach where the water was a little deeper. Here's where the boats were tied up, some for fishing, some for fun. Like at the beach, very few people were out in the heat. The trio walked over the wooden planks until they found the boat they had been instructed to look for.

"Hello," Dr. McNair said.

Erique Sarpong stopped working on his nets and looked up. He wore shorts and an unbuttoned top, and a huge straw hat to provide shade. He stared at the trio with stern eyes, especially at the scuba equipment. He nodded.

"I'm Stephen McNair with the US government. This is Sally and Thomas. We were told you could take us out diving."

Erique shook his head. "I'm sorry, I don't do charters anymore. I'm a fisherman."

Dr. McNair looked confused. He looked at Sally and Thomas,

then back to Erique. "I can pay you well."

Erique looked at his son, Emmanuel, then back to Dr. McNair. "Where do you want to go?"

"No, Papa," Emmanuel said.

Dr. McNair handed him the charts.

Erique stared at the paper. His breathing escalated. "No. I'm sorry. I cannot take you there."

"Why not?" Sally asked.

Erique looked each one of them in the eye before coming back to Sally. "There is something under the water. Something evil."

Dr. McNair turned to look at his companions. He had been so happy, looking forward to doing some fieldwork, but this was certainly putting a damper on it. He looked back at Erique. "I can pay you two thousand dollars for just a few hours of your time."

Erique stood fast and quiet.

"Four thousand?" Dr. McNair pleaded.

Thomas walked up to Erique and extended his hand. "I'm Thomas Freeman. Perhaps you've read my books."

Erique shook his hand but his brow furrowed with confusion. "Your books?"

"Never mind him," Sally said. "We're needing to go here for the same reason you don't want us to. We know there's something wrong out there. We have to find out what it is so no one else will get hurt."

Erique searched her eyes as if deciding if she was being honest. He apparently was not convinced. "I am sorry." He turned his attention back to his nets.

After several seconds of silence, the three turned around to leave. "We'll find another boat," Thomas said.

As they got about twenty feet away, Erique called out. "Wait."

"No, Papa," Emmanuel said again.

"I cannot let them go out there with someone else," he said to his son. "I could not live with myself." He looked back to Dr. McNair, who had walked back to him along with Sally and Thomas. "I

81

will do it, but you must promise me that you will all do as I say. If I say it's time to come back, we come back. Agreed?"

Dr. McNair shook his hand. "Agreed."

They boarded the boat and Erique headed slowly out to sea. He left his son at the dock. As he cleared the beach area, he opened up the throttle and the boat sped toward its destination. An hour and a half later, he stopped the boat. "We are here."

Sally took a depth finder from her gear and mounted it by the controls of the boat. "Can you go back and forth toward the south? We're trying to find something under the water."

Erique nodded and headed south, crisscrossing as he went. About twenty minutes later, the depth finder beeped.

"Stop the boat," Sally said. As he stopped, Sally took out her scuba gear.

"You're going in the water?" Erique asked. "That was not part of the deal. I beg you not to do that."

"I do this all the time," she said.

"I'm telling you," Erique said with a dark harshness to his tone. "There is evil down there. Would you die today?"

Sally looked to Thomas and Dr. McNair.

"Maybe we should come back with submersibles," Dr. McNair said.

Sally scoffed. "I'm going. I don't believe in evil . . . or aliens." She gave Thomas a quick look with that word.

Erique pushed the throttle and the boat started moving. "Let me get you right on top of it. Then promise me you will only go down for five minutes. And be very careful. The current is very strong here."

"Yes," Thomas said. "Watch out for the current, Xie. Get it— currency?"

Sally ignored Thomas and nodded to Erique. "I promise. Thank you." She took off her clothes to reveal a black bikini underneath. As she sat and started gathering her gear, she looked up at Thomas. "You can stop staring anytime."

Thomas smiled. "I'll try, but you are a beautiful woman."

She put on her gear and sat on the edge of the boat. The ocean was very calm as she looked over the edge.

"Remember," Erique said, "five minutes."

She gave him a thumbs-up, checked her regulator, and fell backward into the water.

Erique leaned over the boat and watched.

The gentle rocking of the boat and cool breeze felt good to Dr. McNair. *This is what I've been needing*, he thought.

Erique kept checking his watch every fifteen seconds. He got up and started pacing back and forth.

Thomas walked over and sat by Dr. McNair. "This guy is making me nervous."

Dr. McNair nodded in agreement.

A few minutes later, Sally emerged and swam to the back platform. Thomas helped her into the boat.

"Well?" Dr. McNair asked. "What did you see?"

Sally removed her mask and looked around at the other three. "You're not going to believe this. About two hundred feet down, there is a wall of giant rocks. Must be half a mile high. It is a reef now, but these are not natural formations. They have been placed there over several years, possibly three or more."

"How can that be?" Dr. McNair asked. "How could someone build a wall over a long period of time without anyone knowing? And why would they do it?" He looked over at Thomas, who was nodding as if this verified his theory. "Could it be?"

"Can we go now?" Erique asked.

"No," Sally said. "I want to get a sample of the algae growth to determine how old this wall is." She opened her case and took out a sample bag and positioned herself on the edge of the boat again.

"Five minutes," Erique said once more.

She nodded and fell back into the water.

Erique sat on the side of the boat and breathed deeply.

A few minutes later, Sally emerged with her bag and climbed

into the boat.

"That's it?" Erique asked. "We go home now?"

"No," Sally answered. "I want to see the southern end of this thing. Judging by the satellite views, it runs about a hundred miles."

Erique didn't move.

"I can pay you more," Dr. McNair said.

"It is not the money," Erique said, still looking at Sally. Finally, he returned to the controls, started the boat, and followed the signals of the depth finder for hours until it no longer reported the wall. He traveled back to the area where they picked up the last signal. They decided this must be the southern end of the wall.

Sally sat on the edge of the boat and prepared herself again. She nodded as Erique held up five fingers, then she fell back into the water.

Minutes passed as Erique paced the boat again, which made Dr. McNair nervous. "What happened the last time you were here?" Dr. McNair asked.

Erique looked down as the events of that day replayed in his mind. "I don't know. Something down there scared the dolphins. All I know is, a diver was killed and one badly injured, and it was all wrong how it happened."

"What do you mean?" Thomas asked.

Erique started recounting the horrific ordeal as Thomas and Dr. McNair looked on. Suddenly, he stopped and pointed.

Bubbles had erupted on the calm surface thirty feet behind the boat. Sally's hand breached the surface, but that was all. Erique ran and dove over the side of the boat and swam out to her. Thomas did the same. Dr. McNair jumped over the transom and waited. The two men made their way to the back of the boat, towing Sally's limp body. Dr. McNair held her while the men climbed up and lifted her back into the boat. Her mask was gone and blood was running down from a severe laceration in her neck.

Erique rushed to the front of the boat, started the engine, and sped away. He grabbed the radio and started calling for help. "Mayday! Mayday! We have an emergency."

Dr. McNair tried to stop the bleeding. Sally still had a pulse but was unconscious.

The radio screeched and a voice came back. "What is the nature of your emergency?"

Erique motioned for Thomas to take the wheel of the boat and pointed in the opposite direction of the sun. "Keep it going that way." He squeezed the mic again. "We have a diver badly injured. We can't make it back in time. Please send a helicopter. Our coordinates are twenty-one degrees west by twenty degrees north. I have activated the emergency beacon. We are heading back toward Nouakchott. Please have the helicopter meet us."

The voice on the other end of the radio confirmed. "I'm sending the helicopter now."

Erique rushed back to Sally and Dr. McNair. "How is she?"

"I have stopped the bleeding but she's lost a lot of blood." Dr. McNair kept his hand pressed tightly against her neck. "I hope that chopper finds us soon."

Erique went back to the controls and motioned for Thomas to step aside.

"We should have listened to you, man. I'm so sorry," Thomas said.

Erique kept his eyes on the sky. Twenty minutes passed but seemed like hours. "There!" he yelled.

Dr. McNair looked up and saw the helicopter approaching. Thomas began to wave his arms wildly back and forth above his head. "We're going to make it," Thomas yelled. He stood beside Erique and watched the helicopter getting larger in perspective.

Suddenly something rose out of the water a mere forty yards ahead of the boat. It was round, metallic blue, and shining in the sunlight. It seemed to be twisting as it rose. Erique veered the boat sharply to miss it, but it was too large.

Thomas grabbed the side of the boat and looked back at Dr. McNair. "Hold on to—"

The boat hit the object with a resounding thud. The front of the boat disintegrated on impact as the vessel went airborne. Everything seemed to happen in slow motion from that point as all four passengers flew off the boat and hit the water along with debris from the wreckage.

The helicopter arrived as all four bodies were floating in the water. It hovered.

Thomas saw Sally floating facedown and turned her over. She wasn't breathing so he started administering mouth-to-mouth.

"Is she all right?" Dr. McNair asked.

Erique had gotten to Dr. McNair and was helping him stay afloat. None of them had been wearing life preservers.

Thomas kept his focus on Sally and continued administering CPR. Finally she started coughing and spitting out water as everyone breathed a sigh of relief. Thomas kept one hand tightly on the wound in her neck to prevent more bleeding.

A diver jumped out of the helicopter and swam to them. Another person in the helicopter lowered a cable and basket. The diver and Thomas lifted Sally up first and secured her for the ascent. Within thirty minutes all four were safely aboard and were given blankets.

The diver and the other rescue guy began tending to Sally's neck. "What happened?" one of them asked the others.

"We didn't see," Dr. McNair said, "but it could have been dolphins or killer whales."

The two rescue men looked at each other in disbelief.

The helicopter flew directly to the hospital and landed on the roof. Orderlies quickly took Sally to the elevator. Dr. McNair, Thomas, and Erique waited for the elevator to come back up. When it opened, a familiar face was looking back at them, at least familiar to Erique.

"We're making a habit out of this, Mr. Sarpong, aren't we?"

"Who are you?" Thomas asked.

The tall dark man stepped out of the elevator. "I am Officer Jakande. I cannot believe you would take people out there again."

"Sir, in his defense," Dr. McNair said, "he didn't want to. We talked him into it."

"This I believe," Jakande said. "Get yourselves looked at. I'll be back to get a statement."

11

"You're just so adorable. Yes, you are." Rebecca, Darren's beautiful young assistant at the new SETI command center, rubbed Roscoe under the chin as he excitedly accepted the attention. The neckline of her blouse hung down enough to reveal a black bra.

"You like dogs, do you?" Darren asked while trying to keep his eyes on her face.

"Oh, yes sir, Dr. Mitchell. I sure do. Well, to be honest, I like men who like dogs." Her smile revealed two perfect rows of stunning white teeth.

"Yeah, me too," he said.

She laughed.

Darren blushed. "I mean . . . I like dogs, not men who . . . uh . . . not men."

She laughed harder. "You're cute," she said as she turned her attention back to Roscoe.

Who's cute? Darren wondered. *Me or Roscoe?*

"So how long have you had him?" she asked.

"Ten years."

She nodded. "Did it hurt him when you clipped his ears and tail?"

"Oh, I would never do that," Darren answered. "He was like that when I got him."

"Was he a rescue?"

Darren smiled. "You could say that. I found him living in the woods in Alabama."

Rebecca smiled. "Tell me about it."

"Sure. I was in my last year of grad school and I had gone home for spring break to visit my folks. They live in a very rural area of Alabama on a small farm. Mom told me about this stray dog that they had been seeing, you know, coming around scavenging for food and stuff."

"That's so sad," she said, her full attention now directed at Darren.

"Yes, I agree," he said. "I mean, he was surviving in an area full of coyotes. He was scrawny and so dirty we couldn't even tell what color he was. I knew I had to do something. I told my mom and dad that we needed to catch him and give him a loving home."

"What did they say?"

"They agreed, but my mom thought I had too much going on with grad school to take care of a dog too. She wanted us to catch him and try to find him a home or turn him in to a shelter. But I knew the shelters in smaller towns don't have the resources to handle a lot of dogs, and being a pit bull might move him up on the list to be put to sleep, and I couldn't take that chance."

Rebecca's eyes glowed and she crossed her arms over her chest. "You have a big heart. You saved him."

"Well. He saved me if truth be told." Darren was laying it on thick. "My life got so much better after I took him in. He was so scared at first. He wouldn't go anywhere in my apartment until I carried him there. But he slowly came out of his shell and has become the best dog in the world. He's still afraid of some things, like thunder and lightning, and even rain, but he loves the dog park and being around other dogs."

"You never thought of getting him a little brother or sister?" she asked.

"Oh sure," Darren lied. "I figured once I had a bigger family I would do that."

"So what's keeping you from doing that?" Rebecca added a devious look to that question.

Darren swallowed hard. "I guess I just haven't met the right person. You know it's hard with work and all."

Several seconds passed as they stared at each other until it became uncomfortable.

"Well, can I get you a cup of coffee, sir?" she asked.

"Sure, that would be nice." Darren turned his attention back to his computer as she walked away. "Yeah, that's right, I'm cute," he said to Roscoe. It was great being the boss and certainly something he was not used to.

"Hey, boss."

Darren spun around to see Brian, one of his fellow SETI physicists. Brian's family had moved to the United States from India, and Brian had the look and even wore traditional Indian clothes at times, but had no accent at all.

"Tell me you got something," Darren said.

"Nada." He handed Darren the latest report.

"How is this possible?" Darren studied the sheet carefully. "It doesn't make sense. If we can detect the signal and even determine its level of output, then why can't we tell where it's coming from or how far away it is?"

Brian shrugged. "It's a mystery for sure. We'll figure it out, though. Thanks again for choosing me to be part of the team."

Darren smiled and nodded. Brian was one of the sharpest young minds he had ever met. "What do your parents think of your career choice now?" He remembered Brian mentioning how they were disappointed in his chosen field.

"No improvement," Brian said. "My dad is a neurosurgeon and thinks I should have followed in his footsteps. My granddad was also a surgeon."

"But this discovery is huge. Don't they realize that?"

Brian shrugged. "They said that when I meet E.T., they'll support me."

Darren laughed. The remake of the classic movie *E.T. the Extra-Terrestrial* had hit theaters at the beginning of the summer.

"What about your parents?" Brian asked. "Do they believe in

what you're doing?"

Darren nodded. "Yes, they do. Of course they don't under-stand it. I've tried explaining to them but whenever I mention aliens, they think I work with National Security keeping an eye on Guate-malans."

"Dang, I should have told my parents that," Brian said with a chuckle. "So what's next, boss?"

"Have everyone meet me in the conference room. Let's have a powwow," Darren said. He gathered his notes as Brian went to deliver his orders.

"Here's your coffee, sir," Rebecca said, walking up with the Styrofoam cup in her hands.

Darren shifted his notes under one arm and took the cup. "Thank you." He walked into the conference room and put the cup and papers at the head of the table. He waited as the other six SETI employees joined him, all of them with their own notes.

"Okay," Darren began, looking out over the faces at the table, "let's talk about what we know and what we might be able to deduce from it. Since the signal is mathematical and since they have the tech-nology to send it, I think we have to assume they're intelligent."

Everyone around the table nodded in agreement.

"So the first question is," Darren continued, "why can't we tell where the signal comes from or how far away it is?"

Steven Yuen raised his hand.

"Steven?"

"I'd say it's intentional." Steven looked around the room. "I mean, I'd say they don't want us to know."

Darren nodded. "I'll buy that. That certainly coincides with them being intelligent."

"Not just intelligent," Barbara Long, another physicist, stated, "but possibly hostile."

"What do you mean?" Darren asked.

"Well," she continued, "why the need for secrecy? If they're intentionally keeping us from knowing where they are, how can that be a good thing? Okay, maybe not hostile, but certainly sneaky. The signal was not meant for humans, nor do they even want us to know about it and certainly not to understand it. If that is intentional, then they're up to something."

"I see your point," Darren offered. "That certainly puts it into context. What else is something we don't know?"

"Why the oceans?" Brian asked.

"Very good, Brian," Darren said. "Why the oceans indeed? Any thoughts?"

A woman named Tanisha raised her hand. "Maybe they're ichthyological."

Barbara laughed. "Fish people? That would be cool. Can't wait to see what they look like."

"So they're communicating with their own kind?" Darren shrugged. "Maybe."

Steven spoke up again. "Maybe they have bases underwater, on the ocean floor in the deepest parts. Maybe they've been there a long time."

Darren stared upward as he pondered the possibility. "Or maybe it's a rescue mission for a ship that has gone down in the ocean."

"Yeah," Brian said. "I like that."

Ahmad joined in. "Is anyone else worried that the signal is directed at the oceans when water might be the most scarce and valuable element in the universe?"

The room grew quiet as everyone considered the possibility.

"That would be bad," Brian said, breaking the stillness. "If they came here and robbed us of our water, we would all die."

"So how do we stop them?" Barbara asked.

"This is just a hypothetical," Darren said.

"Okay, then," Barbara said, "hypothetically how would we stop them?"

Steven laughed. "We send a sign up into space saying, 'Welcome to Earth. Don't Drink the Water.'"

Almost everyone laughed.

"They're instructions."

Everyone turned to look at Lucas, the one at the opposite end of the table, the one who never spoke up during these meetings. He was clearly the smartest person among them, which is why Darren had selected him to be part of the group, but he had regretted the decision. Lucas was crude and had offered no insights into the situation. His overly large frame, dirty T-shirts, tight sweatpants, and unkempt beard, which was long and jet black, were a turnoff to everyone.

"What was that?" Darren asked.

Lucas crossed his arms and stared out from under his thick black eyebrows. "Instructions."

"Okay, I got that," Darren said, "but can you explain what that means?"

Lucas sat back with no expression. "The signal repeats itself. It's aimed at the seas where you will find the most intelligent and easily trainable animals on our planet. Whoever is sending the signal is training the mammals of the seas to do something for them."

"What?" Barbara asked.

"I don't know," Lucas said.

Brian nodded. "It makes sense. Let's assume that Lucas is correct. And let's assume that whoever is sending the signal is getting closer. What would aliens from another world need mammals of the ocean to do for them?"

The room grew very quiet as everyone pondered the question.

Steven spoke up. "I've got it. Food. They're coming to our planet for food. They train the fish beforehand . . . uh, I mean mammals. Then when they get here, they hover above the water and lower cages, and the dolphins and whales and such are already trained and swim right in. Then the aliens go back home with tons of fresh seafood."

Darren smiled. "Sounds plausible to me."

"You want another scenario?"

All eyes turned to Lucas again.

Darren nodded. "Sure."

"If any alien race invaded," Lucas began, "what would be the biggest threat to them?"

"Our atmosphere?" Darren asked.

"I'm talking offensively, moron. What would be the biggest military threat to them?"

No one paid attention to the "moron" remark, not coming from Lucas. Plus, they were too engrossed in the question.

"Our navy has a great arsenal with the nuclear subs and massive battleships and carriers. That's our strongest military might," Brian said.

Lucas smiled. "And where do you find those?"

The room was silent again.

"Wait," Barbara said. "You think they could train whales and dolphins to destroy ships and subs? I don't think so."

"I don't know," Brian said. "With millions of them, it could be done."

"I agree," said Darren. "Just like a flock of birds can take down an airliner."

Barbara sighed. "Well, if that's the case, we don't have to wonder about intentions anymore. If that's not proof of hostility, what is?"

Darren corrected her again. "We're just spitballing ideas here. These are just 'what-ifs.' None of it is proof of anything."

"Then maybe we should attack this from the other end of the spectrum," Brian said.

"What do you mean?" Darren asked.

"Let's assume they are friendly," Brian said. "Let's assume a visit would be a good thing. Looking at it from that angle, what would be the reason for the secretive signal aimed at the seas?"

"Very good," Darren said. "Okay, everyone, let's do that. Let's hear any hypotheticals that would coincide with a friendly visit."

After five minutes of total silence, the small group of SETI employees began to see how dim the future looked.

Soon they began to talk about other subjects. They talked for several more minutes until Darren looked up and saw something that made him stop. His boss, Dr. Vincent De Luca, and the director of SETI, Dr. Natalie Zimmerman, stood at the entrance to the conference room. They had strange looks on their faces, which automatically changed the dynamics of the attitudes in the room.

"Hey, come on in," Darren said. "We were just having a brainstorming session. You guys can join in if you like."

Dr. De Luca and Dr. Zimmerman walked to the head of the table. "That won't be necessary," Dr. Zimmerman said. "We have some information for you."

Darren looked at them both with anticipation. "Tell us."

"We've had a call from the Pentagon," Dr. De Luca said.

"The Pentagon?" Darren repeated. "What is it?"

"It's that building in Arlington with five sides, but that's not important now."

Everyone turned again to stare at Lucas.

"Sorry," Lucas said. "Just a joke. Please continue."

Dr. De Luca looked over the room. "Why don't you guys excuse us for a minute and Darren can fill you in later."

The employees grabbed their notes and filed out of the conference room. Brian was the last one in line and closed the door behind him. When they had their privacy, Dr. Zimmerman and Dr. De Luca turned their attention back to Darren.

"Let's have a seat," Dr. Zimmerman insisted.

They all sat down.

"So, tell me. Has the Pentagon learned something new?"

Both Dr. De Luca and Dr. Zimmerman nodded.

Darren was getting excited. "Okay, tell me. Have they learned where the source is and how far away they are?"

Dr. Zimmerman reached over and took Darren's hands in hers, a very odd gesture from her or any scientist, especially one's boss. She squeezed his hands gently and looked him in the eye.

Dr. De Luca slid a manila envelope across the table. "Classified" was stamped in red ink across the front.

Darren pulled his hands away from Dr. Zimmerman and opened the envelope, took out the contents, and began to read. His lips moved as he silently read the papers on top. As he flipped through the stack and read, his eyes got wider and wider. "You mean—"

"That's right," Dr. Zimmerman said. "They're already here."

12

Dr. McNair opened his eyes. From the look of the hospital room, he knew it had not been a dream and they were still in Africa. The room was dark and musky. A doctor and nurse were standing over him. A policeman came in to get a statement.

After he told the officer what happened, and the policeman informed him of the outcome, he was allowed to get out of bed and visit Sally in her room. She was in a coma. They had bandaged her neck, but she had lost a lot of blood and swallowed a lot of seawater. Dr. McNair felt tears run down both cheeks as he stared at Sally while the respirator pumped air to her lungs through the tube down her throat. He thought back to his wife and daughter. He always felt like his work had pushed them away, but the guilt was much worse now. It was his direct actions that led to the current situation. He had been so ready to have one last adventure that he had not considered the danger, even when Erique had made it clear.

Several days passed. He was released from the hospital's care with minor abrasions and contusions. But he wouldn't leave, waiting only for Sally to hopefully come out of the coma. After several days, she finally woke.

When the doctors concluded that she was going to be okay, Dr. McNair approached her. Her eyes lit up when she saw him. The tube was still down her throat so she couldn't talk. She took a marker and wrote on a legal pad and turned it to face him. It read, "Are you okay?"

He nodded as tears ran free once again. "I'm fine."

She scribbled again. "Erique?"

97

Dr. McNair nodded. "He's fine."

"Insurance?" she wrote next.

Dr. McNair shrugged. He hadn't even thought to ask Erique if he was covered for the damage. The damage of course being that his boat was totally destroyed.

The next note made him laugh.

"Goofy?"

"He's fine as well. He waited around hoping you would wake, but he finally had to go back home. They say you're going to be fine. Should be out of here in a few days. You should know that Thomas saved your life. You were clinically dead and he revived you with CPR. Well, like I said, I thought you should know."

She nodded. Then she wrote again on a new sheet. She turned it around. "Are you saying his lips were on mine? YUCK!"

Dr. McNair laughed. But her next message made him gasp as he stared at the three-word sentence. It read, "I saw them."

Sally told him everything via notes and he believed her.

The next day, Dr. McNair took a taxi to the waterfront and asked the driver to wait. He walked the familiar path down the dock to where Erique's boat was docked before. There was nothing and no one there. He found another fisherman and asked if he knew Erique. He did and told him where he lived.

Dr. McNair walked back to the taxi and gave the driver the address. Fifteen minutes later, the taxi pulled up to a very small cinderblock house. There were a couple of old cars on blocks in the front. There was no grass at all. The yard for this house and every house in the neighborhood was pure dust.

The cab pulled away without waiting as Dr. McNair walked up to the door. He knocked.

Emmanuel opened the door.

Dr. McNair smiled.

Emmanuel turned and yelled back into the house. "It's the man, Papa."

Erique came to the door and looked confused but was hospitable. "Come in, Dr. McNair. Please come in."

Dr. McNair followed Erique to the small kitchen and sat at the little wooden table when prompted.

"This is my wife, Leena," Erique said.

"It is my pleasure to meet you," Leena said. "Can I get you something to drink?"

Dr. McNair nodded. "Some cold water would be great."

She smiled and went to the fridge.

"How is the woman?" Erique asked.

"She's fine," Dr. McNair answered. "We're going back home soon. I wanted to come by and see if you were okay."

"I was not hurt," Erique said.

"I didn't mean physically," Dr. McNair said.

Erique looked confused.

"I meant financially," Dr. McNair clarified. "Did you have insurance on your boat?"

"It does not matter," Erique said. "I would not go back out there if I could."

"Really? You seem very much at home on the water."

"Maybe once," Erique said. "But things have changed. The ocean has changed. It is not a place for people anymore."

Dr. McNair nodded. "What will you do?"

"I will go to work for my father. He is a roofer. There is much work here now."

Dr. McNair turned up the glass of water and drank it all. "You will miss it, you know?"

Erique smiled. "Yes, I will. A love for the sea is part of a person's soul. I will always love her." He looked at his wife and son. "But some things are more important."

They sat and talked a little while longer until Dr. McNair left to go back to the hospital.

Three days later, Dr. McNair rolled Sally out of the hospital in a wheelchair and helped her into a taxi. As the driver pulled into traffic, Sally's cell phone beeped.

"Thomas," she said, holding up the phone so Dr. McNair could see the name associated with the text. Opening the message, Sally giggled. "Can you believe this guy?" She handed Dr. McNair the phone.

"Oh my goodness," Dr. McNair said with a chuckle. "Is that a pit bull puppy?"

Sally took back the phone and looked at the small screen. The picture message was of Thomas holding up what appeared to be a pit bull puppy and the text read, *Here's your get well present.*

"You know, he's not a bad guy," Dr. McNair said.

Sally smiled. "I guess he has a few good points."

They both laughed.

Two weeks later, Dr. McNair and Sally sat on the bench waiting to be called. They sat motionless, Dr. McNair occasionally wiping the sweat from his brow. He looked over at Sally, who wore a pant-suit similar to the one she was wearing the day they had met, a bandage still around her neck. She had almost fully recovered from the accident and was now waiting to address the Congressional Oversight Committee, which made decisions on various matters including global warming. They had already received her report, and now she and Dr. McNair had to explain it.

The door opened and the same middle-aged woman appeared. "Doctors, they're ready for you."

Dr. McNair and Sally walked to the table and took their seats in front of the raised platform where the five senators were poised and ready for their interrogation. Dr. McNair noticed that the room wasn't empty this time. In the rear, barely visible, sat a small man, almost bald, wearing rim glasses. Dr. McNair wasn't sure why the man was there.

Senator Elaine Biddle from Arkansas began. "We've read your report, Dr. Xie, and frankly, we don't understand it."

"Which part do you not understand?" Sally asked.

Senator Weingold from New York spoke up. "To be honest, it reads like a terrible Hollywood movie script. One has to wonder if this was something that came to you in a coma-induced dream."

"I assure you, Senators, this was no dream." Sally looked at Dr. McNair for support.

Dr. McNair stood. "She's telling you the truth, no matter how hard it is for you to believe. We all heard her describe the wall before she was attacked. It is even visible from satellite photos, so it's quite real."

"We have seen the photos, Doctor," Senator Butler confirmed. "We believe the wall is real; it's just the builders, the creatures who you say are building the wall—that's what's hard to swallow."

Sally borrowed a line from Dr. McNair. "All I can do is report the facts; it's up to you to decide what to do with them."

"You want us to believe that they possess that kind of intelligence?" Senator Biddle asked. "You're saying that whales, orcas, and dolphins, and every mammal in the sea, have been secretly building a one-hundred-mile-long wall of rocks in the ocean. And they're doing this to change the flow of ocean currents?"

"That's correct," Sally said. "Whales bring in the giant rocks in their mouths and drop them. Smaller mammals arrange them in place. I saw it with my own eyes. That's why they tried to kill me."

Senator Malcolm from North Dakota spoke. "And you believe this is causing global warming?"

Sally nodded. "It's making the ocean current go a hundred miles farther south before turning northward. It's almost reaching the equator now. That makes it pick up much warmer water before heading north. That's the reason the Gulf Stream has been so warm, why we've had stronger storms, and why the ice caps are melting so fast. Along with harnessing warmer water, thousands of whales now travel the current all the way to the northern ice caps."

"I don't understand that part," Senator Butler said. "What does that do?"

"Mammals are warm-blooded, Senator," Sally explained. "With so many following the current, they manage to keep the temperature a couple of degrees warmer than it would normally be."

101

"I don't get it," Senator Weingold said. "Why? What is their motivation?"

"We don't know," Dr. McNair said. "While it would benefit sea life greatly to kill off every human on the planet, the warmer climate doesn't help them in the long run. We think maybe they've been trained to do this."

The senators looked back and forth at each other.

"A mad scientist perhaps," Senator Weingold said with a chuckle.

"Maybe," Dr. McNair said, taking the steam away from the intended sarcasm. "We don't have that information. But the information about the wall, the current, and the climate is all real. Frankly, I thought the committee would like this news."

Senator Biddle looked at him. "You realize this means all of your former reports are wrong, don't you?"

Dr. McNair smiled. "I do."

"Then why would we like this news?" Senator Butler asked.

"Because," Dr. McNair said, "it is news that you can all agree on. We don't have to stop drilling for oil, or buying it from the Middle East, or stop doing anything you claim hurts the economy. For the first time, we have a tangible problem that can be dealt with." Dr. McNair began putting Sally's papers back in her briefcase. This was his signal to the committee that they were finished. Sally followed him toward the door.

"One more question, Doctors."

Dr. McNair and Sally stopped and turned around.

Senator Malcolm continued. "Do you think this has anything to do with the alien invasion?"

Sally laughed.

"What are you talking about?" Dr. McNair asked, knowing Senator Malcolm was not the kind of person to joke. In fact, she was the only one on the committee whom he respected.

"Have you not watched the news lately?" Senator Weingold asked.

Dr. McNair glanced at Sally, then back to the panel. He walked a little closer. "No. What has happened?"

"Just rumors so far," Senator Butler answered. "But the rumor is that aliens have landed in Central America and are setting up shop."

Dr. McNair shook his head. "I haven't heard anything. But as to a connection with what's going on in the ocean, I couldn't possibly say."

As the two left the building and walked out into the sunlight, Thomas, who was waiting for them on a nearby park bench, jumped up and ran over. "Well?"

Sally shrugged. "It's like talking to a brick wall. I don't think they believed any of it."

"Have you guys heard about the alien invasion?" Thomas couldn't control his enthusiasm.

Dr. McNair laughed. "We just heard. What do you know?"

Before Thomas could answer, a marine in uniform walked out of the building. "Are you Dr. McNair, sir?"

"Yes, I'm Stephen McNair."

"Will you please wait right here, sir?"

Dr. McNair nodded. The marine disappeared back inside the building. A couple of minutes later a young man wearing a jacket and tie, and quite uncomfortably it seemed, rushed out of the building.

"Dr. McNair?" He rushed up to them and bent over to catch his breath. It was the small man who had sat in on the meeting before the oversight committee.

"It's okay, son," Dr. McNair said. "Take your time."

The young man finally caught his breath and stood up. He took off his rim glasses and used his tie to clean them. "I hate suits. Sorry." He placed the glasses back on. "I'm Dr. Darren Mitchell with SETI."

"SETI?" Thomas yelled. "Hey, how are you?" He was obviously glad to find a kindred spirit.

"Sorry," said Dr. McNair. "He's our alien expert, Thomas

Freeman. What can I do for you?"

"Thomas Freeman?" Darren repeated.

"That's me," Thomas said, shaking Darren's hand. "Perhaps you've read my books."

"Yes, yes, I have," Darren said. "All of them. The last one, *Mark My Words: They're Coming,* is my favorite. I'm a huge fan."

Thomas stood there in a daze while Sally and Dr. McNair laughed.

Darren released Thomas's hand and looked at the others. "Uh, I need your help. I'm in charge of putting together a team for a situation that has unfolded, and I need experts in several fields, including climatology."

"Is this a government project?" Dr. McNair asked.

"You could say that," Darren answered.

Dr. McNair looked at Sally and Thomas. "Well, we're a team. You don't get me without these guys. Sally is a marine biologist."

Darren smiled. "I'll take you all. Follow me and I'll brief you along the way."

"Don't tell me," Sally said. "This is about the alien invasion, I suppose?"

Darren opened the door to the building they had just left and held it for them. He looked each one in the eyes and then answered. "Yes, it is."

13

Colonel Benjamin Jamison sat on his sofa waiting for his wife, his neatly pressed jacket hanging over the back of the sofa so as not to get wrinkled. Angel, his pit bull, sat beside him. It was Sunday morning and he and his wife were heading to church. The television was on but he was paying no attention. Instead, he was staring at the family picture atop the TV, the one with him, his wife, two sons, and much younger daughter. He smelled his wife's perfume as she walked up behind him.

"I'm ready," Belinda said as she brushed lint from her dress. She looked up at the TV. "What are you watching on the news? Are they talking about aliens?"

The colonel laughed as he looked back to the screen. "Yes, I believe so. They've been doing a lot of news stories recently about aliens."

"Is it real?"

"Come on. It never is. Probably a publicity stunt to lure tourists."

"I have your robe," his wife said.

The colonel shook his head. "You don't really expect me to go through with this?"

Belinda stood firm. "Yes, I do. I'm tired of people saying you're not friendly. You used to love to sing in the choir before—"

The colonel didn't argue anymore. He knew she was right and knew what she was trying to say. Ever since his daughter drowned in the family swimming pool ten years ago, he had become withdrawn. He had cried harder than he knew he could that day, but not one drop since. He wasn't sure if he could anymore. Nothing seemed to matter in life. His two sons were grown now, one a second lieutenant in the army and one a veterinarian, and he couldn't remember the last time he had spoken with either of them. His faith was about all he had left, and he often questioned that, wondering if he was just going through the motions.

He took the robe, and he and his wife went to the door. Angel followed and watched them leave. They got in the car and drove to church.

On the way, he turned on the radio, but after hearing more about aliens, he quickly turned it off and wondered how there could be so many gullible people in the world.

Twenty minutes later they arrived at the small church just off the army base where the colonel was stationed. He dressed in his robe, his head and burly forearms the only things visible. His formidable appearance belied the fact that he wasn't a very tall man; he was slightly under six feet. He joined the choir, ready for the first song.

The congregation of the small church swayed back and forth to the rhythmic sounds of the choir, like lilies dancing in a warm summer breeze. Colonel Jamison held his hymnal and let his baritone voice soar among the other choir members. His neatly shaved dark head glistened in the light and was almost motionless as he sang. He occasionally glanced up to see his wife, who was seated in the pews. Belinda was still a beautiful woman, her shining black hair cut short and accented now by streaks of silver. Her face was still relatively free of wrinkles, except when she smiled as she was doing now. He knew she was his strength; she always had been.

It was a humid summer day in Georgia as the morning sunlight burned through the stained-glass windows, casting distorted replicas along the far walls like artistic abstracts of holy scenes. Suddenly, both double doors in the rear of the sanctuary opened. Two men in full dress uniform entered, several medals adorning the left breasts of their jackets. They stood motionless and stared at the colonel.

The colonel looked up and noticed them. Adrenaline rushed

106

through his body. He was in the back row of the choir, so he closed his book and quietly stepped backward off the platform and disappeared.

Belinda looked confused until she turned and saw the two soldiers. Her head dropped.

Moments later the colonel appeared from the back in just his suit. He had removed the choir robe. He strolled down the center aisle as the choir continued without him. Belinda was sitting at the end of a pew and held her hand out as he passed. The colonel gently caressed her hand as he walked on toward the soldiers, who quickly stood at attention as he neared. He nodded and followed them to the black car waiting outside.

"What is this about, gentlemen?" he asked as they drove away. He looked beside him at the driver and to the backseat at the other soldier.

"Sorry, sir," the one in the back said, "we don't have that information. We were only sent to retrieve you. Do you know, sir? Is it about the aliens?"

The colonel scoffed, then sat silently, looking straight ahead. The last time he was "retrieved" like this was when his CO informed him he was going to the Middle East. But there were no current wars and none brewing, at least none of which he was aware. As the car passed the entrance to the base, the colonel realized they were driving him to his home. He knew what that meant.

As the driver stopped on the curb in front of his house, Colonel Jamison got out and went inside to pack. He stuffed all his essentials into a duffel bag, put on his dress uniform, and walked back through the house, stopping in the living room to stare again at the picture on the TV. He took a deep breath and continued. "Come on, Angel," he called out. His older pit bull quickly rushed to join him.

He opened the back door and Angel jumped inside and began licking the soldier in the backseat. Colonel Jamison took the front seat again. Once inside the car, they drove to the base and directly to the airfield. A small vehicle like a golf cart took them from there.

Angel enjoyed the ride. They drove past several hangars until they reached the one they were looking for. A three-hour helicopter flight later and Colonel Jamison found himself and Angel being driven to the Pentagon.

An escort took him from the car to a guarded room. The colonel removed his cap and looked at the marine guard. "I'm here to report."

"Yes, sir. They're expecting you." The guard opened the door.

The colonel handed the guard the leash to Angel. "She needs some water." The guard looked confused, but he nodded. Colonel Jamison was more tired than curious now as he entered. He saw his old friend General Nickerson, who was also in full dress, so he walked up and saluted.

"At ease," the general said after returning the colonel's salute. "Come on over, Benjamin."

The colonel noticed several other people in the room. Two were wearing black suits, and, judging by their demeanor, he guessed they were agents. Another was a smaller guy with rim glasses, then an older man, an Asian woman, and a hippie.

"Colonel Jamison, these gentlemen are with the NSA," the general said, motioning to the agents. "And this here is Dr. Darren Mitchell with SETI."

"SETI?" the colonel asked.

The little guy got up and walked over with his hand extended, which the colonel shook. "Search for Extraterrestrial Intelligence. We're the weirdos always trying to find intelligent life from beyond this world."

The colonel smiled. "When you find some on this planet, let me know."

General Nickerson laughed and walked over to the large conference table and sat at one end. "Let's all take a seat. Benjamin, I'm sorry I had to pull you out of church."

Colonel Jamison and Darren sat on one side and the two agents, Dr. McNair, Sally, and Thomas all sat around the table. The colonel waited for them to brief him.

"Benjamin," the general said, "what have you heard about this alien invasion?"

The colonel tried not to smile. "I've been hearing it on the news for about a week. I kind of figured it was a hoax."

"It's not."

The general's quick response and stern tone gave the colonel alarm.

The general looked to Darren. "Tell him what we know."

Darren turned in his chair to face the colonel. "A few weeks ago, six large spikes of unknown material sped toward Earth and penetrated into the beaches off each coast of northern Panama, each measuring over two hundred feet high. They had writings of an unfamiliar language on them and we weren't even sure at the time where they came from." He reached into his briefcase, pulled out a picture, and handed it to the colonel. The pictures showed the spikes in great detail.

"And you say these objects have been delivered by aliens?" the colonel asked no one in particular.

"That's right," the general said.

Darren handed the colonel another picture. "And here's where they came from."

The colonel looked at the picture but didn't see anything. "It's just empty space."

Darren nodded. "Yes, that's what we thought. This image was captured by the Hubble. But if you look at this area here," he said, pointing to the photo, "you'll see an area of distortion."

The colonel looked hard. "Okay, I see it. What is it?"

"A spaceship of some kind," Darren said. "It was able to approach Earth, possibly taking a year or more, and still was not detected. It uses a type of ambient energy to refract light, making it invisible to the naked eye and to radar. It settled into an orbit above Central America. Once we knew where to look, we found it. We estimate it to be a perfect sphere about twelve hundred miles in diameter."

"And they dropped these spikes?" the colonel asked.

He nodded.

"Why?"

"That's the sixty-four-dollar question, isn't it?" the general asked.

"We weren't sure at first," Darren said, "but we know now. We think they're settlers."

The colonel turned to look at the general as if expecting him to explain this was a joke. He did not.

The general looked at the agents. "Show him the pictures."

"Those are classified," one of the agents said.

"Show him!" the general said in a louder tone.

The agent reached into his case and brought out a large manila envelope, which he slid across the table to Colonel Jamison.

The colonel held the large envelope in his hands and searched the faces of all at the table. "Let me guess—little green men?"

"Nope," the general said, "large white ones."

The colonel opened the envelope and removed the stack of pictures. The first one took his breath away. It was an alien, humanoid in appearance, but huge. The body was pure white. The legs were muscular but shorter in proportion than a human's. The arms were longer and bulging with muscles. The head was hairless and large, its jaws larger than the cranium, displaying a huge mouth. It wore only a simple garment that covered half the legs and torso, leaving the arms fully exposed. The colonel stared for a long time before looking up. "So, you're telling me that Earth has been invaded by albino steroid freaks? Are they friendly?"

Every other head at the table shook in unison.

"Hostile?" the colonel asked.

"Very," the general said. "This is just one of their workers. Go to the next picture to see one of the soldiers."

The colonel moved the current photo to the bottom of the stack and stared at the next. The creature was the same, only wearing

110

body armor, which covered it from its ankles to its neck. It seemed to be carrying a weapon that looked like a simple piece of wood.

"These guys came in and cleared the entire area that the spikes outlined," Darren said.

"The entire area of north Panama?" the colonel asked.

The general nodded. "Yes, and it only took them a few days. They terminated every living thing in the area without prejudice."

The colonel looked hard at the picture. "It looks like the armor only covers the front. Maybe we can use that if we can get behind them or make them run."

"Maybe," said the general, "but making them run might prove difficult. A large group of drug dealers took them on and it was a slaughter. The alien's weapon is far more advanced."

The colonel looked back at the picture and pointed to the object the alien was carrying. "Are you talking about this two-by-four?"

General Nickerson smiled. "Yes. That two-by-four apparently shoots pure energy and holds approximately twenty-five shots before needing recharging."

"What does that mean—pure energy?"

"It means, Benjamin," the general said, "they pull the trigger here, and three hundred feet away the ground explodes like it was hit by a grenade. Anything or anyone in that blast radius is taken out."

The colonel looked to Darren for verification. He was nodding.

"After they cleared the area of all people and animals, the tops of those spikes illuminated and a protective shield was generated. Only then did the working crews come in," Darren said.

"That's right," the general agreed. "The soldiers simply returned to their transport on the ground for some R & R while the workers used huge dozers and pushed the trees and foliage aside, all the way to each coast. Then large machines were brought in and they started erecting these structures." He motioned for the colonel to look at the next picture.

Colonel Jamison stared at the photo, which clearly showed the huge buildings already erected. They were complete with doors and windows, and some had huge objects on top that resembled satellite dishes. "So they're moving right in, are they? Is that it?"

Everyone nodded.

"And judging from the size of their ship," the general said, "they might go all the way through North America before they're finished, maybe the entire planet."

The colonel knew the next question was crazy, probably even moot, but needed to be asked. "Have we tried communicating with them?"

Darren nodded with a solemn look on his face. "Yes, we tried. We have a symbol language based on math that should be universal to any intelligent being. We sent three representatives down to try this approach. The workers simply ignored them and when the shield opened, the soldiers . . . well, it didn't work, that's all."

"Have they moved beyond this initial area?" the colonel asked.

"That's right," one of the agents said. "Once this area was completed, which only took a couple of weeks, more spikes fell to the north and the soldiers returned to clear the new area. Trust me; it was much easier this time since almost everyone had fled. The shield then moved northward using the new spikes. The southern point of the shield remains stationary. In other words, the entire operation is slowly headed this way."

"They're only advancing northward?" the colonel asked.

The general nodded. "That's why we need to stop them. The president and Congress have authorized a deployment. I want you to lead this defensive effort. Dr. McNair, Dr. Xie, Dr. Mitchell, and uh . . . Thomas here will be your advisors. You'll also have marines, regular army, National Guard, and a garrison of the Mexican Army at your disposal. I need you, Benjamin. I need someone who can focus."

The colonel wondered what that meant but didn't ask. He had been a successful strategist in the Middle East a decade ago, and had heard the rumors that he didn't care if he lived or died. He didn't remember wanting to die, but life had taken on a different meaning after the loss of his daughter. But an alien invasion was a different animal altogether. He wasn't exactly thrilled to be chosen for this mission, but it was his duty. He replied the only way he knew how. "Yes, sir."

14

The steel projectile flew on its own power, its short wings stretched out on each side, a steel dragon waiting to breathe its venomous fire upon impact with its target.

"The nuclear missile is en route, Colonel."

Colonel Jamison stared down at the wallet in his hand, the picture section flipped open as his thumb traced the outline of the tiny face on the faded snapshot. The summer sun shouted down from heaven, each syllable assaulting the men in uniform until dark sweat stains betrayed every pressed shirt. A drop of sweat fell from the colonel's forehead and landed on his thumb, the bubble of perspiration neither rolling off the rough texture nor being absorbed into the dry skin, as he continued to caress the face in the picture.

"Colonel?"

He looked up and acknowledged the man. "Thank you, Lieutenant."

Lieutenant Williamson nodded, then motioned to a viewing screen on a portable monitor. "We can watch it here, sir."

The colonel positioned himself in front of the screen but continued looking at the picture in his wallet. He was very broad, and the fatigues only added to his imposing image. A dimple in his generous chin accessorized his chiseled face. Twenty-five years and two wars during his stint as an army officer had hardened him, inside and out, which was augmented by the loss of his daughter. He took the hand with the wet thumb and wiped away the sweat that had accumulated on his scalp, where a whisper of salt-and-pepper color announced the only hair on his head.

"Was that your daughter, sir? I mean . . . is that—"

"It's okay," the colonel said as he smiled to reassure the lieutenant. "Yes, this was my daughter, Victoria. We lost her ten years ago. She was four years old."

The lieutenant, a tall, slender Caucasian man with pointed features and short black hair, nodded. "Is that why you volunteered for this assignment?"

Colonel Jamison looked up in surprise, but he had heard those rumors also. "No, son, I didn't volunteer. I'm just here to do my duty—same as the rest of us."

It was hardly an assignment for which to volunteer, perhaps even a suicide mission, but something had to be done if the invasion were to be stopped before reaching the United States. As each area was cleared, more spikes fell from the sky, each time farther north. After each area was completed with new constructions, the alien soldiers returned to clear the way for the workers. To date, nothing had stopped their progress.

Colonel Jamison stared at the screen, the image being provided from long-range cameras on a destroyer in the Caribbean Sea. He could make out the camps of the aliens and see the creatures walking casually about as if they didn't have a care in the world. The colonel hoped that was about to change.

The metal monster, which had been launched from a Stealth Bomber, sped toward the southern face of the shield. It had been determined that this would be the safest point to detonate a nuclear weapon, since there were no people in the area that had already been claimed. Nicaragua and Costa Rica were now void of humans, and in the southern part of Panama, over 1.5 million people had been evacuated.

"Impact in fifteen seconds," the lieutenant said.

The colonel took a deep breath. He closed his wallet and returned it to his pocket. He watched the screen with hope. The missile connected with the shield in a brilliant paroxysm, white plumes of poisonous smoke frothing outward into the sky.

"Did it work?" the colonel asked, trying to see through the bright aftermath of the blast.

As the view cleared, it became apparent that the shield had not been damaged at all. The aliens had not even stopped what they were doing to glance upward at the attempted destruction.

"I'm sorry, sir," the lieutenant said.

The colonel nodded. He reached into his back pocket and pulled out a pack of Red Man chewing tobacco. It was unopened. As he pulled the top apart and the glue released its grip and the plastic keep-fresh zipper lock spread wide, he thought about the last time he had a chew. It was ten years ago as the war in the Middle East came to a close. That was 2040. He chewed tobacco only when he was at war, and the failure of the nuclear missile just assured him that was his current status. As he placed a wad of the moist dark leaves in his mouth, he immediately felt comforted as the flavor spread through his flesh and along his veins. "How many days before the shield lifts and their soldiers advance?"

"Headquarters predicts two days, sir."

"I want to see them," the colonel said. "Get me a jeep."

"Yes, sir." Lieutenant Williamson quickly walked away.

The colonel looked left and right at the line of defenses. It was the first time the military had gone back to the woodland camouflage colors since the wars over seven decades ago. But the sand-colored uniforms wouldn't work here in Central America. That point might be moot since it seemed the enemy had infrared sight, possibly from their mother ship. In the videos he had seen, they always knew where people and even animals were hiding, and eradicated them easily.

As he looked at the faces in his line of sight, he noticed everyone was waiting, although he could see the anxiety in every face. The northern front of the shield now ran almost perfectly along the line where Honduras and El Salvador bordered Guatemala. About twenty miles from the shield, thinly stretched almost two hundred miles from coast to coast, were 100,000 US Marines, 200,000 soldiers of the US Army, 50,000 National Guard members, and another

75,000 members of the Mexican Army. Along with 800 tanks, 200 Apache helicopters, a dozen aircraft carriers in the Pacific Ocean and Caribbean Sea, and at least 10 nuclear subs, the colonel felt confident they could stand their ground against the bigger and more technologically advanced enemy. And if not, they would sure put on a show of firepower.

The lieutenant pulled up in a jeep. "Ready, sir?"

The colonel climbed into the passenger side and the lieutenant navigated along a dirt road through the dense foliage. The windshield was down and the air hitting him in the face brought little appeasement from the sultry atmosphere. Thirty minutes later they came to a clearing and could see the area marked with paint to signify the invisible shield up ahead.

The lieutenant pulled up within twenty feet and stopped. They both got out and walked up to the shield. The alien machines were visible from there. The colonel took his field glasses and zoomed in on the busy scene.

"They're huge."

The lieutenant nodded. "Yes, sir, over eight feet tall."

The colonel marveled at the workers. They looked like giants of fairy tales. They walked upright just like humans, and with all the same parts, but their skin was like leather: tough, thick, and completely white, just like he had seen in the photos. But seeing them in person was something else. They looked like deformed Greek gods. The facial features provided perhaps the most dissimilarity to humans. There were only holes in the sides of the broad heads for ears, and the eyes, nostrils, and mouths were all larger in proportion. And in two days, the soldiers, who were even larger, would emerge from this shield with full body armor, massive guns, and even more massive egos. The colonel spit a large blob of tobacco juice onto the shield. It made a slight sizzling sound as it oozed down the side.

"What do you think, sir?"

The colonel didn't want to tell him what he thought. He didn't even want to think it. "Let's get back," he said.

117

As they arrived back at camp, the colonel called for a meeting with the other commanders and advisors, which included Major Strafford from the US Marines, Captain Owens from the National Guard, and General Echevarria from the Mexican Army. He had them meet him in the mobile command center.

"This is nice," Thomas said as he looked around the command center with its computers and communication devices.

"*Shhh,*" Darren said.

As they sat around the table waiting for the latest word, the colonel reached into a duffel bag and pulled out an old unopened bottle of scotch.

"Ah yes, 1972," the colonel said as he held it up and offered it to the group. "A gift from General Nickerson."

"Is it that grim, Colonel?" Major Strafford asked.

Colonel Jamison chuckled as he looked at the major while pouring him a drink. He knew the major well, mostly by reputation. His scarred face seemed to be a testament to the rumors of him being an authoritative warhorse. They had certainly chewed on some of the same dirt a decade ago.

After everybody had a drink, it turned serious. "What's the plan?" Captain Owens asked.

Colonel Jamison looked at everyone in the room before answering. "We have got to show them that the property of this planet is not free. If their MO doesn't change, just before the shield rises, they'll launch new spikes about ten to fifteen miles north. We have planes that will fly over and mark that line with dye. That will be the enemy's goal—to clear that area and build on it. We will be right in between and our goal is even simpler: keep them from obtaining this new ground. As soon as the shield begins to rise, battleships will hit the area with everything they have, followed by fighter pilots from the north, and an Apache regiment will come up from behind. If that doesn't stop them, well, that's where we come in."

Major Strafford laughed very loud, which didn't set well with the colonel. "Permission to speak freely, sir."

"Speak your piece, Major."

The major still spoke as if choosing his words carefully. "I just want to be sure I understand. You're saying that if fifty-caliber shells from the battleships, Tomahawks from the fast-movers, and Side-winders from the choppers don't stop them, then we are supposed to do it with tanks, rocket launchers, grenades, and M16s?"

The colonel smiled. When he put it that way, it didn't make much sense. He could see the worry in the other commander's eyes. "We're hoping they'll get the picture and rethink using Earth as a settlement," the colonel added. "But if some do get through, then yes, that's what we hit them with."

"Colonel?"

The colonel looked over to General Echevarria. He was a tall dark figure whose face, like Major Strafford's, advertised his experience, and his eyes were as dark as his thick mustache. "Yes, sir?" Even though it was agreed that Colonel Jamison would be in charge, he still respected the higher rank.

The general spoke calmly, using perfect English, his body so rigid it looked as if his neck muscles didn't work. "The major has a point. It's great to hope that the initial assault is successful, but what if it fails completely and we are advanced upon by the full force of the alien garrison?"

The colonel looked around the room. Major Strafford was expressionless. Captain Owens, however, was a ball of uneasiness; his eyes conveyed the disquietude of the others clearly for all to see. Yet, unlike the others in the command center, Captain Owens looked like he could have just as easily been coaching a Little League baseball team.

The colonel thought about it. He knew they were right. "Okay, I want every jeep and truck parked behind the line of tanks, pointed in the opposite direction. If the retreat order is given, everyone heads north and regroups past the spike line." He looked around the tent. "Is that clear?"

The general and captain nodded, but the major was silent.

"Is that clear?" the colonel repeated.

Running away was not in the major's blood, but he obeyed the order. "Yes, sir, crystal clear."

The colonel looked over to Darren. "This is Dr. Mitchell with SETI. He discovered the signal the aliens were trying to hide. These other people are all experts in their respective fields and are here to provide any intel or advice that might help us complete our objective. Dr. Mitchell, tell us everything we know so far."

Darren nodded. "Well, everyone, we believe this colonization has been in the planning works for several years. The signal we discovered has been live for at least that amount of time, although we just discovered it recently. These aliens are very intelligent; that much we know. They were training the mammals of the oceans to build a giant wall of rock that diverted the Gulf Stream farther south to the equator, which has been causing the acceleration of the melting of the ice caps and causing the global temperatures to rise."

All eyes were glued on Darren as he spoke.

"Anyway," Darren continued, "we know they prefer warmer weather than humans. That's probably why they chose Central America. Plus, the narrow land possibly gives them a tactical advantage.

"But as you can see from the pictures, they appear to be humanoid. We believe that makes them susceptible to the same extremes. The body armor suggests they are also vulnerable to injuries or death if their bodies aren't protected."

"Have any of them been killed so far?" Major Strafford asked.

Darren shook his head. "None that we've witnessed."

"Okay," Captain Owens said. "We know they're here to set up a settlement. But we don't know how much area they need or want. Right? I mean, what if they only want a small section to occupy? Would that be so bad? Maybe they'll keep to themselves. Maybe we can learn a lot from them."

Darren wasn't sure what to say, so he looked to Thomas. "Uh, Mr. Freeman here is the authority on this, so I'll turn it over to him."

This caught Thomas off guard, but he cleared his throat and

thought about how to word his statements. "If you look at the history of our own world, you'll see a pattern that is pretty universal. When a more advanced civilization settles in an area already occupied by a less advanced culture, it inevitably leads to the eradication or exodus of the less advanced culture and people. Even if these aliens were to stop with the area they've accumulated so far, we would not be safe. What happens when they start to multiply, or begin to run short of resources? It might take years or even decades, but at some point the human race will just be in their way and the easiest thing would be for us to disappear. They see Earth as their colony now, and nothing is going to change that. And again, this is assuming they stop spreading right now. We have to consider the distinct possibility that they have their eyes set on a much larger area to begin this colonization."

The entire room was silent. Sally was impressed and patted Thomas on the arm.

"That makes sense to me," Major Strafford said. "Either we deal with them now or later. My vote is for now."

Colonel Jamison nodded and rose from his chair, and the others followed. "It's settled, then. We make a stand now. Let's go to work, everyone."

15

The sun was getting low in the sky like a giant, dull flashlight casting the remaining efforts of light from a set of drained batteries. The jeep bounced along the rugged terrain. Lieutenant Williamson drove without looking over at the colonel, his own thoughts no doubt reliving the events of this dreadful day.

Colonel Jamison took out his wallet and flipped open the pictures and began tracing his thumb along the contours of Victoria's face. A drop of blood fell from his forehead and landed on his thumb. A shadow from above crossed his lap and he looked skyward to see an eagle, or perhaps a hawk, soaring freely low in the western sky. He put away his wallet and took out his pack of chewing tobacco. It was half empty. He put a stash in his jaw and savored the flavor, not seeming to mind that it was mixed with sweat, dirt, and blood. He looked in the side mirror of the jeep at the scene behind him—the battlefield. The view was black as hundreds of trails of smoke lifted upward to feed the huge cloud hovering overhead. It looked like a storm full of tornadoes.

"The command center has moved a little farther north, sir."

The colonel looked over at the lieutenant. His shirt was covered in blood, most likely not his own. The colonel had watched as the lieutenant pulled at least seven wounded soldiers to the jeeps. He would surely recommend him for a medal. He had witnessed many acts of bravery this day, but the battle was decidedly one-sided. No, not one-sided—a massacre.

As the jeep stopped, the colonel got out and walked toward the command center, blood now steadily dripping from his head. He moved slowly, every muscle and joint hurting.

"I'll get a medic," the lieutenant said, motioning to his own head but referring to the colonel's.

Colonel Jamison smiled but didn't say anything. As he entered the command center, Angel rushed to greet him. Her wagging tail made the colonel feel better. "Hey, girl. Did you miss me?"

Major Strafford and Captain Owens were both as beat up and bloody as the colonel. They both quickly stood at attention and saluted. The colonel returned the salute. "At ease."

"She's been whining for you all day," Sally said, pointing to Angel.

"Thanks for looking after her."

Sally smiled.

Thomas brought the colonel a bottle of cold water. Colonel Jamison responded with a nod. Everyone found a seat.

"Where's General Echevarria?" the colonel asked. "Did he make it?"

Darren nodded. "He's with his men. Trying to convince them not to run away."

The colonel pulled out the bottle of scotch and laughed. "He might need to convince me too."

This broke the tension as they all laughed hard at their own situation.

The lieutenant entered the command center with a medic and pointed to the colonel. The colonel didn't resist as the medic began to clean the wound on his head.

"What happened to the initial attack?" the captain asked. "How did they survive that?"

The lieutenant shook his head. "According to reports, they were able to deflect the shells and missiles, everything we sent at them from the air."

"It was part of their main shield," Darren said. "Like an umbrella."

"What are the losses, Lieutenant?" the colonel asked.

The lieutenant looked at the floor before answering. "We lost over thirty percent of the men, sir. They took out every single tank and half the helicopters. The aliens are already clearing the new area, dozing trees and bodies alike to each coast."

That news hit the commanders hard.

"So," the colonel said, "they couldn't take out the fast-movers. Maybe we can use that."

"I don't see how," the major said. "They are well protected from any attack from the air."

"Sir," the lieutenant said, "General Nickerson wants an update."

The colonel didn't move. He waited until the medic finished wrapping his head, then slowly rose out of his seat, with effort, and hobbled over to the SATCOM. He nodded to the lieutenant, who walked over and operated the device until they had General Nickerson on the line.

"What's going on down there, Benjamin?" the general asked.

"We got our butts kicked, General. That's what's happening."

The open line buzzed and cracked for a few seconds before the general spoke. "It's your call, Colonel. If there's nothing more you can do, you make the call to come home."

The colonel looked around the room. Captain Owens was shaking his head. Major Strafford's jaws were clenched in defiance. General Echevarria entered the tent and seemed to sense what was happening. He nodded and gave a thumbs-up.

The colonel cleared his throat. "We're not ready to tuck tail just yet, General. I want napalm."

"You got it, Colonel," the general said with enthusiasm. "How much do you need?"

The colonel clutched the transmitter tightly. "All of it. And we need replacements. Every soldier you can send."

"Well, all right," the major said as Colonel Jamison and General Echevarria took their seats and the lieutenant and medic left the tent. "What's the plan, sir?"

The colonel looked them all in the eye, one at a time, and continued. "They were able to deflect the attacks from the ships and planes, but once they get away from the shield, they can be hurt. I saw one take a direct hit from a tank and he went down. He was still kicking, but I never saw him get up again. What did you guys witness?"

"We took out several with rocket launchers," the general said.

Captain Owens concurred. "Same here. We had a little luck slowing them down with grenades, but the M16s had little or no effect. The frontal armor is just too strong."

"We did pretty well with claymores," the major added.

"Okay," the colonel said, "we know we can hurt them. The problem is that we're no match for them with conventional ground combat or weapon-to-weapon. They're too strong, too fast, and their weapons are much more advanced." He slid a map to the center of the table and pointed. "Here's the shield now. It runs from the lower point of Belize right through Guatemala City. We're here, approximately twenty miles away. We'll let them get within a few miles of us, far away from their shield, and drop a thousand tons of napalm on them. It should hurt them or at least disorient them. Then we hit them with everything."

All of the commanders nodded and went to spread the word.

Over the next two weeks, as the aliens cleared the new area and built their new structures, troops and equipment came pouring in.

"Do you want us on the front line, sir?" a newly arrived captain asked.

The colonel smiled. "Son, that's all we have. We have security and medical personnel behind us, but every soldier is on the front line."

The captain nodded and began positioning his men.

"Walk with me, Dr. Mitchell," the colonel said.

Darren left Dr. McNair, Sally, and Thomas and walked with the colonel.

"You guys are here to lend advice," the colonel said. "So, I'm

125

all ears."

"We've got nothing, colonel. These creatures are totally un-precedented. I wish I could tell you their weakness, but they don't appear to have one. I think your plan of attack sounds like the best bet."

Lieutenant Williamson walked up. "Sir, we have a situation." He motioned toward the back about a hundred feet away where the security forces were.

The colonel saw the commotion and walked directly toward it. Darren followed. As they walked up, they saw a standoff between the security guys and what appeared to be a Mexican gang. They were a hundred strong, all wearing gang paraphernalia, and all carrying Uzis and other such weapons. The colonel walked right up to them. "What's going on, Sergeant?"

"These guys are trying to get through, sir."

The colonel looked at the one who appeared to be the leader. He was barely out of his teens. A faint mustache and goatee ac-centuated his taut face. He was short and thin, with dark eyes and olive skin. He wore a sleeveless shirt, and his arms displayed several tattoos of demons. The colonel rubbed his own shirt and could feel his cross necklace just below his dog tags. "What's your name, son?"

"Francisco."

Darren's eyes lit up. "Colonel, I know him."

Colonel Jamison walked up close to Darren. "What do you know about him?"

Darren smiled. "He saved my life and my dog's life. He loves pit bulls."

"That's all I need to hear." The colonel walked to Francisco and held out his hand. "I'm Colonel Benjamin Jamison."

Francisco seemed surprised at the civility and shook the colo-nel's hand.

"What can we do for you, Francisco?"

"We came to fight, sir."

The colonel looked out at the other faces. All were nodding.

He thought about how best to handle the situation. "Do you know what we're up against, Francisco?"

Francisco nodded. "Yes, sir. And I know if we don't stop them, our homes and families will be next. Not everyone in Mexico can afford to fly to another country."

The colonel nodded. "Those weapons might not be too effective on their own." He turned to the lieutenant. "Get these men some rocket launchers and grenades and show them where to set up."

The gang members cheered and followed the lieutenant.

"We need all the help we can get, Sergeant," the colonel said.

The sergeant smiled. "Yes, sir."

Darren returned to the command center as the colonel walked back to the front line and watched as everyone worked to get ready. The newcomers had heard the horror stories, and the fear was reflected in their faces. He wished he had words to offer for comfort, but Colonel Jamison couldn't quell his own trepidation.

The estimated day arrived and the new spikes sped downward. Everyone waited. The colonel watched the monitor as the alien soldiers rushed outward from the raised shield. With no attack imminent, they ran with ease toward the waiting soldiers. Marines had marked the point for attack where claymore mines lay waiting. The aliens kept coming. As they neared the American and Mexican troops—and gang members—the colonel gave the order to charge. Everyone started running forward, snaking southward through the brush. Fighter jets flew over and began to drop napalm, but like all other attacks from the air, it was deflected. The sky lit up in bright red as the napalm connected with the shield above the aliens. The claymores worked. They caught the enemy off guard and at least disoriented them for a while.

As the explosions began to subside, the colonel and his men arrived to bombard the aliens with grenades and rockets. It worked better than the last defense, but only temporarily. Some aliens were down, but as the remaining alien soldiers regained their composure, they opened fire with their large guns. Each shot opened a hole in the ground with a massive explosion, sending any soldier within ten feet flying into the air.

But no one gave up; everybody just kept throwing grenades and firing the rockets and rifles.

Colonel Jamison knew they had made a decent stand today, but without proper firepower, there was nothing more they could do, so he gave the order to retreat. That proved to not be an easy task. The aliens reacted to the new attack with a vengeance, firing at will at anything moving.

Soldiers rushed to the trucks and jeeps to get away. Some trucks were totally destroyed by the alien fire. The colonel hurried to a jeep as Lieutenant Williamson joined him. They sped away, trying to make it to the dye line that marked the new territory. But they didn't make it. A shot from an alien gun connected with the back of the jeep and sent it airborne.

The colonel found himself on his back twenty feet from the impact crater. His eyes were blurry, his ears ringing. He could move, albeit not without pain, but he concluded nothing was broken. He tried to stand but couldn't. As his eyes began to focus, he saw the beast coming toward him. He turned and looked northward and could see the dye line only about twenty yards away. There was no way he could make it.

The giant alien did not appear to have his weapon, so he charged the colonel with the apparent intent of simply squashing him, his eyes glowing red.

The colonel pulled his sidearm and fired at the face of the alien. It had no effect. This was it. He was helpless. Suddenly the armor of the alien erupted in two explosions, throwing him off balance. Someone grabbed the colonel underneath the arms and began dragging him. He was pulled all the way past the line through the dye. As soon as he was on the other side, the alien, who had recovered from the grenade blasts, did not pursue any farther, but turned to stroll away.

The colonel looked around expecting to see Lieutenant Williamson. But such was not the case. When he saw the identity of his rescuer, he smiled.

"Are you okay, Colonel?"

The colonel felt over his body. He was beat up, bruised, bleeding, and sore, but very much alive. He nodded to the guy who had pulled him to safety. "I'm okay, Francisco." He looked over the young man who had just saved his life. Any other time he would have frowned upon such a person, maybe even looked down on him. For some reason, his fatherly instincts, which had eluded his own sons for so long, kicked into high gear. "Where's your mother and father, son?"

Francisco shrugged. "Never knew my father. My mom and younger sister are at home."

Without trying to sound condescending, the colonel attempted to express his concerns. "Don't you think you should be trying to take care of them instead of running around with a gang?"

Francisco looked the colonel in the eyes. "*Sí.* I do try to take care of them. I know that being in a gang was my choice, but I assure you, Colonel, it wasn't my first choice."

As the colonel looked into Francisco's eyes as well, he knew now he had never tried to understand. How could he know what this young man had been through in his life? How could he judge him by his appearance? All he knew for sure was this person showed up and volunteered to put his life on the line for his family, and that he had just pulled him to safety. He knew there was only one appropriate thing to say. "Thank you for saving my life."

The young man smiled, stood up, and lowered his hand to aid the colonel, who took his hand and stood up as well.

"*Sí*, Colonel. You're welcome."

16

Colonel Jamison sat at the table in the command center, now positioned in the southern part of Mexico. It had been two days since the last battle. Although they had mounted a more successful defense, losses were still great, totaling 30 percent of manpower once again, except for the Latino gang, who never heeded the retreat order and continued to fight, even taking on the monsters hand to hand. As far as the colonel knew, there were only about fifteen of them left, including Francisco.

"Sir?"

The colonel glanced up, obviously unaware that others had joined him. "What is it, Dr. Mitchell?"

"I'd like to call a think session."

The colonel looked up wearily. "What is that?"

"It's what we used to do at SETI meetings. We throw out ideas at random, hoping one will be of use."

The colonel nodded. "Yes, let's do that."

Everyone sat around the table. General Echevarria, Major Strafford, and Captain Owens seemed eager to hear any ideas.

"Okay," Darren began. "Let's begin with what doesn't work."

Major Strafford laughed. "That's quite a list."

Colonel Jamison nodded. "We know every attack from our ships, subs, and fighters and bombers have been unsuccessful, even the napalm. In other words, our most powerful weapons are null and void."

"Okay." Dr. McNair joined in. "So we have to concentrate on what will work on the ground."

Everyone nodded in agreement.

"How about bear traps?" Thomas blurted out.

All four military commanders laughed.

"No, that's okay," Darren said. "This is exactly what a think session is. Not all ideas pan out, but the key is to keep throwing them out there."

"If only they were allergic to something," Sally said. "You know, something not harmful to humans."

"Maybe we could examine one of the dead ones," Captain Owens suggested.

"Exactly," Sally said. "If I could do an autopsy on one of them, we might learn something about how their systems work."

"But the shield covers the battlefield when the fighting is over," Major Strafford said. "That means we'd have to attempt that during the heat of battle. How would we even do that? Hook a rope around their ankles and drag them to you?"

"It might work," the colonel said. "Let's try to figure out a way to get a dead alien to Dr. Xie so she can dissect the bastard to find out what makes him tick."

Everyone nodded in agreement.

"Back to the question at hand," the major said. "How do we fight them now?"

"What about bees?" Thomas asked. "Maybe we could drop a hundred hives on them. Even if they weren't allergic, it would sure be painful to them. I mean . . . wouldn't it? "

"Now that's not bad," Major Strafford said.

The room was silent for two full minutes as everyone thought.

"Well," the colonel finally said, "are bees and bear traps the best we've got?"

"The truth is," Sally said, "that primitive weapons might be the most effective. Their technology is so far advanced, they've learned how to defend against high-tech weapons, but maybe they've forgotten how to defend against low-tech devices, even bear traps."

Captain Owens spoke up. "The same goes for us. We can't train soldiers overnight how to use spears and bows and arrows again. I mean, if that's what you're suggesting."

"Even spears and arrows won't penetrate their armor," Major Strafford said. "We need something that can attack them from behind."

"Boomerangs," Thomas blurted out again.

Everyone laughed.

"It's not bad," the colonel said. "Do we know of anything more lethal that can circle around to the rear of the aliens?"

No one had an answer.

"Wait a minute," Dr. McNair said. His eyes shifted around but were not focusing on anything in the room. "Wait a minute," he repeated.

"Well?" Darren said. "Share it with us."

Dr. McNair looked up. "I was just remembering my family's last ski trip many years ago."

Everyone laughed.

Captain Owens patted the table as he laughed. "Great. Do you have slides?"

"No, no, wait," Dr. McNair continued. "I remember that it hadn't snowed so the resorts made their own. These creatures love the heat, right? They've been warming our planet for years now. They even picked Central America for their point of invasion. Forget attacking them with fire from above; let's attack them with cold from the ground."

The colonel sat up a little straighter. "How would we do that?"

"Snow machines," Thomas said.

The colonel let the information sink in. "You mean—"

"Yes, sir," Dr. McNair answered. "We set up snowmaking machines all along the front of the shield and blast away. I'm not sure the snow will stay with this heat, but it might cool the area down enough to make them really uncomfortable."

The colonel jumped up and rushed to the SATCOM and put in a call for General Nickerson. Once he got him on the line, the colonel told him what they needed.

Major Strafford crossed his arms and nodded. "Yeah, I knew I would think of something."

The next day, large military helicopters began delivering snow-making machines. They raided every ski resort in North America. Soldiers had instructions to spread the machines out along the front of the shield, approximately one hundred feet away. They worked night and day to finish.

"They're all in place," Sally told the colonel.

The colonel looked out over the area. It was still partially wooded, so he couldn't see very far. But the snow machines were all pointed in the right direction, and it would be only a few days before the shield would lift. To the colonel they resembled large spotlights. "Fire 'em up!" he ordered.

The machines, fed by water lines, came to life and began shooting arcs of snow into the air all the way to the shield. But with temps over one hundred degrees, the snow was melting as fast as it was flying.

"All we can do is let them run," the colonel said and walked back into the command center.

He and the other commanders went over strategies while the team of advisors tried to think of other ideas. They all went to sleep that night with the slightest spark of hope. The snow machines might be a dumb idea, but it was at least an idea.

The hum of the machines allowed the colonel to quickly drift to sleep. He slept long and hard with no nightmares and woke up refreshed, although a bit embarrassed that it was almost nine in the morning. The smell of coffee lured him into the main part of the command center, and he took a seat. Everyone else was already there.

The major laughingly looked at his watch, making the colonel smile.

"One more day after today," the colonel said. "Are we ready?"

"Yes, sir," the major, captain, and general answered.

"Have you looked outside?" Sally asked.

The colonel looked up as he was raising the cup of coffee to his lips. "No. Why?"

Sally and the others were grinning, so he walked to the door and opened it.

"Well, I'll be a monkey's uncle." Angel rushed out beside him and ran toward the machines. The colonel stepped out and let his eyes take in the scene. It looked like a winter wonderland. The ground was covered with at least a foot of snow. It was even piled up on the shield. Angel bounced up and down as she ran and played in the frosty white flakes.

Everyone came outside and laughed at the pit bull having fun in the snow.

"We didn't get much snow in Georgia," the colonel said. "She's loving it."

"Come on," Thomas said to Sally. "Let's play in the snow."

Sally hesitated for a moment, then added another shirt and put socks over her hands. No one had thought to bring winter clothes. Why would anyone, in the summer during a global warming crisis in Central America? She walked out and saw Thomas drudging through the powdery piles of fine ice. She ran to join him.

"Hey!" Thomas yelled as a snowball hit him in the back of the head. "Watch the hair."

"You poor baby," Sally said as she threw another.

Angel bounced all around them as the snowball fight ensued.

Darren and Dr. McNair joined them, and for at least a moment, all of them forgot what a predicament they were in.

"You seem quite at home in the snow," Darren said to Sally.

"You bet. I grew up in Minnesota. We had the harshest winters in all of the country. My parents are still there."

"Ah, the parents," Thomas joked. "I guess you'll be taking me home to meet them when this is all over."

Sally laughed and threw another snowball at him. "In your dreams."

Dr. McNair mostly played with Angel. It made him think of

his new friend, Glenda Eagle. He wanted to forget what lay ahead also, but found it impossible to do so. As much as he enjoyed seeing the accumulation of snow and everyone having fun playing in it, he couldn't help but realize that they were fighting a race of aliens, aliens who had conquered space travel and the harness of solar power, and they were fighting them with flakes of ice.

Throughout the day, the soldiers also tried to forget what lay ahead and played in the snow as well. They made snowmen, had snowball fights, and even made ice cream from the snow.

As the heat rose during the day, it melted some of the snow, but not all of it. Over the next night, it accumulated even more. By the morning the shield was expected to rise, there was at least two feet on the ground and a huge bank of snow piled up on the shield.

The command center was moved north beyond the dye line, and the colonel watched with binoculars as the alien soldiers lined up behind the shield to await their next incursion. He smiled as he watched them stare up at the snow on the shield in confusion. When the alarm sounded and the shield rose, the snow came crashing down right on top of them.

At first they didn't move. They just stood there covered in snow. Finally, they shook off the white powder and began to advance slowly through the knee-deep drifts.

The colonel had the men form the front line much closer to the shield this time, hoping to catch the creatures in the snow. He gave the order to advance. Jeeps sped forward and men rushed toward the enemy. It was working. The aliens were having trouble hitting anything with their weapons.

The colonel and Francisco had remained behind this time. The colonel stood up in the jeep watching the battle through his field glasses. He turned toward Dr. McNair and Sally, who were with the others behind the dye line, and gave a thumbs-up. "It's working!" he yelled. "They're actually shivering."

The aliens still stood in the snow trying to aim their weapons, but the cold was definitely having an effect on their motor skills.

Drivers steered their jeeps right into the snow, spinning and sliding in all directions as they bombarded the awestruck monsters with rockets and grenades. Then the jeeps would pull away before the aliens could react and circle around for another attack.

It was working better than they could have hoped. The colonel gave Francisco the word for them to join the battle. Francisco gritted his teeth and put the jeep in gear. They sped toward the scene.

The snowmakers continued to spit the plumes of powder onto the battlefield. Before long, the aliens noticed this as well and began targeting the machines. By midday, every one of them had been destroyed and the heat of the day was melting the snow fast.

By the afternoon, the entire area was a muddy mess, and the tides had turned. The aliens, no longer cold, began to hit their targets and the troops were forced to fall back. Most of the jeeps and soldiers were completely covered in mud, which had begun to dry into cakes on their skin, making it hard to move. The battle raged on until it became clear that the soldiers had little left to give, so the colonel gave the order to retreat.

Once all the soldiers and jeeps were past the dye line, the aliens simply turned to walk away. Their job was finished after all. They only needed to make the area safe for the workers.

Colonel Jamison watched as they disappeared into the forest. There were several straps across the creatures' backs to support the frontal armor, but no real protection at all. "We have got to find a way to attack them from behind," he said mostly to himself.

"Here, Colonel." Sally offered bottles of water as the colonel and Francisco entered the command center.

"Thank you," they both said.

"I'm sorry it didn't work," Dr. McNair said.

"I wouldn't say it that way," the colonel said. "It definitely slowed them down in the beginning. They sure didn't know what to think of that snow. Plus, they were shivering." The colonel smiled as he thought of the large creatures shaking in the snow. His smile quickly disappeared, however, when he thought about how many soldiers he saw fall this day.

"I don't think we can round up many more snow machines," Thomas said. He looked at Darren and Dr. McNair. "Is there any other way to produce that effect?"

"What about fire extinguishers?" Sally asked.

"We would have to get awful close to use those," Francisco said. "I'd prefer something we could use from a distance."

Major Strafford came into the command center with a severe cut on his arm. It had been bandaged in the field, and not very well.

"I'll call a medic," Sally said.

But the major held up his hand to stop her. "I'll be fine. What are the losses, Colonel?"

"I don't have that info yet," the colonel said. Then he looked around the room and noticed it was much more empty than normal. "Where is everyone?"

17

With another report of high casualties, the colonel ordered all soldiers with young clildren to return home.

"Just the parents?"

The colonel looked up at Major Strafford, then at Thomas, Dr. McNair, and Darren, who seemed to be thinking the same thing. Captain Owens and General Echevarria had not survived the last battle; neither had Lieutenant Williamson, much to the colonel's dismay. He realized now that the lieutenant was one of the bravest soldiers he had ever seen.

"What are you asking, Major?"

"With all due respect, sir," the major said, "what else can we do here? It's been almost two weeks and they have sent no replacements . . . again."

The colonel thought about the question. It was a valid question to which he had no real answer. "What do you suggest, Major? Should we evacuate all of Mexico? Send them to the US? Then what? Send everyone to Canada? If they keep progressing through Canada, then what? That should liven up the immigration debate."

The major didn't laugh at the attempted levity. "I don't know, Colonel. All I know is I've lost more men than I care to think about, and we still haven't even slowed them down, much less made them stop. I realize losing men means nothing to you. I know that's why they chose you for this mission."

The tension was so thick in the command center it could be cut with a knife. Sally looked to Dr. McNair in shock. Thomas was unusually silent.

Dr. McNair broke the stillness. "Hey, we're on the same team here, guys."

The colonel stared at Major Strafford as his words sank home. He wondered himself if that might be true. He looked down at his bloody boots. He could only think about what would happen if they pulled out. How far would the aliens go? What was to stop them from killing everyone in North America, or even the world? What if they never stopped?

"Okay," the major said, as if sensing the colonel's concerns. "Are we getting any replacements or not?"

The colonel shook his head. "They want to reserve the remaining forces in case the aliens reach our border. They are considering reinstituting the draft. Russia and England have decided to sit this one out unless the aliens come to them. The Canadian Mounties have offered their assistance."

The major let out a sad, hopeless laugh. "Well, that's something. When do they expect the shield to rise again?"

"Tomorrow."

The major stood and saluted. "Then I guess we better get ready, sir." He turned and walked out.

The colonel sat motionless. He was being torn apart inside. A part of him knew they couldn't leave, and another part wondered how he could ask men to stay and fight without a chance to win. He pulled out the cross on his necklace and stared at it as if it could provide the answers.

The SATCOM buzzed. "Colonel Jamison? Are you there? Pick up, please?"

The colonel walked over and grabbed the transmitter. "Colonel Jamison here."

"Colonel, this is General Nickerson. I don't think there's any more you can accomplish there, but it's your call."

The colonel thought long and hard. He thought about his wife and grown sons. He thought about his friends and their families. He thought about Victoria.

"Benjamin, are you still there?"

"I'm here, General. Give me one more day."

The general's voice was calm but urgent. "Okay, Colonel, but then I will order you home. We have to consider the possibility that they will reach the US. We have to prepare for that contingency."

"Understood, sir."

"Hold on," the general said, "there's someone else here who wants to speak with you."

That puzzled the colonel as he wondered who it could be. He listened carefully.

"Colonel Jamison? This is President Patterson. Can we stop them or not?"

The colonel smiled. A personal call from the president of the United States was indeed an honor, but hardly practical. "I really don't know, sir. We're giving them everything we've got, but it doesn't appear to be enough."

"What can I do, Colonel?" the president asked.

Colonel Jamison squeezed the transmitter and stared again at the cross still in his hand. "Pray, sir. You can pray."

The hour was late so the colonel lay down to rest, but the demons wouldn't make it easy. Every time he drifted off, he could see soldiers being killed by the aliens or female soldiers being carried off like prizes. It was early morning before sound sleep finally embraced him.

"Sir? Sir?"

The colonel finally opened his eyes. His whole body hurt as he tried to focus. The morning light was already flooding the command center, and he realized he had overslept. His view cleared and he saw the person trying to rouse him. It was Francisco.

"Sir, the new spikes have landed."

The colonel sat straight up and jumped out of bed. They rushed outside. As least now they were clear of the dense forest, and the area in front of them was clear as far as the eye could see.

"Is everyone ready?"

Francisco shrugged. How could they be ready? They had few men and hardly any weapons left. He looked to the colonel as if longing for guidance, or possibly inspiration. None was forthcoming.

The colonel followed Francisco. The other commanders were with their troops, but Darren and the other two scientists—and Thomas—were waiting for him beside a jeep. He noticed a large black box mounted on the roll bar.

"What's going on?" Colonel Jamison asked.

"We're going to try something," Darren said.

"Great. Hit me with it."

Darren nodded. "I don't know if it will work, but we've rigged several jeeps with these large speakers. I've converted the signal the aliens used to manipulate the sea mammals into audio. If we send it back to them, it might confuse them."

"It can't hurt," Thomas said.

"I agree," the colonel said. "It can't hurt."

A soldier rushed up to them. "They're coming, sir."

Everyone looked and saw the creatures coming through the line of trees into the clearing. The colonel gave the order to advance. He got in the jeep to drive himself this time. Darren reached over and activated the recording, and the speakers started blaring out the aliens' own signal. Other speakers could be heard down each direction of the front line as more drivers did the same.

Francisco hopped into the passenger seat with a rocket launcher and nodded to the colonel.

As they sped away, Darren's group stayed outside the command center this time since, for the first time, they could actually witness the battle. They watched as the distance between the aliens and soldiers narrowed. The aliens stopped running and looked at each other as the audio from the speakers reached them. For a moment it did confuse them, but only for a moment.

The earth erupted with the impacts from the weapons of the aliens and the rockets and grenades from the soldiers. Soon the air was filled with black smoke. Darren and the others watched with horror as jeeps were totally destroyed and soldiers fought to their deaths.

"Oh my God," Sally said. "I can't watch this." She ran back into the command center.

But the men couldn't turn away. Dr. McNair and Darren had never imagined how horrific war could be. Thomas was a marine and knew what it was like; still, nothing prepared him for this.

The battle raged on. Francisco and the colonel had evolved a strategy of moving as fast as possible to evade the enemy fire. After all, a moving target is harder to hit. It worked better than anything else, and the other military drivers followed the pattern.

Francisco reloaded the rocket launcher and held on to the roll bar beside the speaker. He aimed and fired a direct hit. The alien went down hard.

But as many successful attacks as the soldiers could muster, there were many more losses for each one. The aliens kept the momentum advancing toward the new spikes, which were only a hundred yards from the command center.

Then it all went south. Colonel Jamison's jeep was hit. Both he and Francisco went flying through the air. They got up and started to run back toward the spike line, but they were soon pursued by two of the aliens, and they were gaining on them.

"Run! Run!" Darren shouted.

Sally stuck her head out the door to see what was happening.

"They're not going to make it," Dr. McNair said.

"The hell they're not," Thomas said. He jumped in another jeep and started the ignition. Dr. McNair jumped into the passenger's seat and they sped away.

Suddenly Angel rushed out the door of the command center.

"Oh no!" Sally shouted. "Angel, come back! Please come back."

Angel ignored her and ran in the direction of the jeep.

Thomas had been paying attention and sped left and right as he drove into the battle zone toward the colonel and Francisco, who were still making a run for it. As they got closer, Thomas realized he was too late; he wouldn't have time to stop and pick them up before the aliens reached them, so he changed his plan. He got to the colonel about the same time as the first alien.

"Buckle up!" he yelled.

"Oh crap," Dr. McNair said as he realized what was happening. He quickly fastened his seat belt just as Thomas rammed the first alien head on.

The alien went down hard and didn't move. The jeep flipped several times and came to a stop upright. Francisco and the colonel rushed to help their friends. They managed to free the seat belts and extract Dr. McNair and Thomas, who were relatively unharmed.

As they turned to run, however, the other alien stood between them and their destination. The creature raised his massive arms out to each side in a display of power. He didn't have his weapon, but he wanted to make it clear that he didn't need it.

Francisco fumbled around searching for a weapon and brought a switchblade knife out of his pocket.

Thomas stepped in front of him. Looking back at Francisco, he smiled. "Didn't anyone ever teach you not to bring a knife to an alien fight?"

Francisco laughed. Dr. McNair and the colonel burst into laughter as well.

This seemed to aggravate the alien even more as he ripped off his helmet and roared. Then he advanced.

"He's mine," Thomas said, ripping off his shirt and revealing a very muscular upper torso. Thomas was an amazing sight for a human, tall and very well built, but he looked puny next to the alien. Still, he met him face to face.

The alien looked down on Thomas with his shining red eyes and charged.

Thomas stepped aside and threw a punch that landed flush on the alien's jaw.

"Come on, Thomas, you can do it," Francisco cheered.

The next punch was not successful, and the creature grabbed Thomas around the throat and easily lifted him high into the air.

143

And then Angel was there. She bit into the alien's legs, the back side where there was no protection, and began shaking her head violently. There is a misconception about pit bulls, that they have locking jaws. It isn't true, but the jaws of a pit bull are extremely strong, as the alien was learning firsthand. The alien dropped Thomas and cried out in pain. He tried to grab Angel but she was too quick. The alien turned to run away but Angel followed, attacking him at will.

Francisco, Dr. McNair, and the colonel picked up Thomas and headed back toward the dye line.

"Come on, Angel!" the colonel yelled.

By now Angel was a long way away, still in hot pursuit, still attacking the alien with ease. She heard the colonel and turned to run back. Other aliens had come running to help the one in distress and fired their weapons at Angel. But she was too fast and their shots landed behind or beside her.

The colonel signaled the retreat, and the orders were passed along via radio to the other commanders. The soldiers made their way back to the north. The alarm sounded and the aliens retreated as well.

By the time the shield activated at the new spikes, everyone was across the line.

Francisco helped the colonel to the command center. "I'll get you a medic."

"No," the colonel said. "There are a lot of soldiers worse than me. Go make sure they're taken care of."

"Yes, sir," Francisco said and left the command center.

Darren and Dr. McNair took a seat in the command center as Thomas went to get a new shirt. A few minutes later, both Thomas and Major Strafford entered the room.

"I heard you boys weren't satisfied to sit this one out," the major said with a grin.

Thomas shrugged. "What are you gonna do?'

"Are you all right?" Sally asked, looking at Thomas. She began cleaning a wound on his forehead.

"I'll live," he said with a smile.

"You saved all our butts," Dr. McNair said.

"That's a fact," Colonel Jamison agreed. "You're one brave man."

Sally smiled at Thomas as she bandaged his head. Then she thought of Angel running out of the command center and felt a pang of guilt. "I'm sorry about Angel," Sally said to the colonel. "I didn't mean for her to get out."

The colonel laughed as he stroked the back of his dog. "Don't be sorry. She also saved our bacon."

Thomas stood up. "She did. Did you see how she attacked that alien? He was helpless. Heck, they couldn't even shoot her."

"Is that right?" Major Strafford asked.

"That's true," said the colonel. "And she's old. I didn't even know she could move like that anymore." The colonel began to look over her body, carefully running his fingers through her short fur. "She doesn't seem to have any injuries. Amazing."

"Is that blood around her mouth?" Sally asked.

The colonel nodded. "Yes, but it's not hers. It's alien blood. Now we know they bleed like we do, and red blood."

"She really got the best of one of the alien soldiers?" Darren asked.

"That she did. Didn't you, girl?" The colonel took a damp cloth and began to wipe the blood from Angel's mouth area. "I wish we had a thousand of her."

Dr. McNair jumped to his feet and stood beside Thomas. Everyone looked at him with confusion as he fumbled for his wallet.

"What is it?" Sally asked.

Dr. McNair looked at the colonel. "How long before the next battle?"

"Usually about two weeks while they build their new homes. Why?"

Dr. McNair found what he was looking for. It was the card that Glenda Eagle had given him with her phone number. He turned

145

the card toward the colonel and then toward the major and smiled. "You want a thousand of her? I can get you more than that. That's right, Colonel, Major, you've just gotten your reinforcements."

Everyone stared with wide-open eyes as Dr. McNair explained about all the shelters just in Southern California alone with thousands of pit bulls.

"It's the same here in Mexico," Francisco added. "And I have a friend who can contact them all."

After listening intently, the colonel was 100 percent behind Dr. McNair's plan. He went straight to the SATCOM. After a few minutes, he got the person he wanted.

"This is General Nickerson. Is this you, Benjamin? Tell me you have good news."

Colonel Jamison smiled as he gripped the transmitter. "I'm not sure if it's good news, but we have a plan."

"Tell me," the general said in an eager tone. "What do you need from me?"

The colonel looked around at the others in the command center before answering. "I need every cattle and sheep trailer you can get. I need as many tankers filled with water as you can send. I need a hundred large fans. I need a thousand large plastic containers. And I need as much dog food as the government can afford."

"Are you serious?" the general asked.

"I'm serious," the colonel said.

Thomas tapped him on the shoulder and raised his eyebrows.

"Oh," the colonel added, "and plenty of chew toys."

"Has the heat finally gotten to you, Benjamin?" the general asked.

The colonel laughed, then explained to the general what had happened during the battle.

"Ah hell, Benjamin, it sounds good to me."

"All right then," the colonel said. "Now can you put someone on who can connect us to a phone line?" With that he turned and looked at Dr. McNair. "Now it's up to you."

18

"I can't believe I'm here with you on my day off," Marcus Olazaba said. "I could be fishing. Heck, I'd rather be back at work."

Glenda Eagle smiled. "Nonsense. This is much more fun than being a cop."

Marcus shook his head. "You are loco."

"There she is," Glenda said. "See her?"

Marcus stared through the openings of the old dilapidated buildings. The wind whistled and tumbleweed blew across the terrain like in an old Western movie. "Okay, I see her."

A person had phoned the Pit Stop and given them info on a stray pit bull. Sergeant Olazaba was simply visiting Glenda and her dogs when the call came in. She quickly recruited him. She knew him to be a dog lover, especially when it came to pit bulls, and she had already talked him into adopting three of hers.

"Come on," Glenda said and walked slowly toward the dog.

It was a big brown female, and the low-hanging teats meant she probably had a litter around. The pit got more nervous as Glenda and Marcus got closer. When they were only about twenty feet away, the pit bull turned to walk away.

Glenda held her hand behind her back. "Give me a cheeseburger."

Marcus took one of the fast-food burgers and gave it to her. She unwrapped it and tore off a small piece.

"Here, girl. Look what I got."

The pit bull stopped and turned around. Glenda tossed the first piece almost all the way to her. The dog quickly swallowed it.

Glenda tossed another, but not quite as far. The dog approached them and gulped down the second piece. This continued until the pit was a mere five feet away.

Glenda sat down and motioned for Marcus to do the same. This made them look less threatening. After several more minutes of coaxing the dog and tossing valuable food, the pit got close enough for Glenda to get a leash around her. She didn't try to run away.

"She wants attention, doesn't she?" Marcus asked as he ran his hands over the dog's head and behind her ears. "Okay, let's take her back."

"We can't," Glenda said.

"What? Why not? I thought that's what we were doing."

"It is," Glenda said, "but she has pups around here some-where. We need to find them too."

"How do we do that?"

Glenda smiled at Marcus. "We let her go."

"Are you serious? After all we went through to catch her?"

"Yep." Glenda nodded. "If she trusts us, she'll take us right to her pups."

Glenda took off the leash, and the big pit bull mom just stayed right there with them. "Let's walk around," Glenda said.

So Marcus and Glenda wandered around until the pit bull walked away from them. They followed her, and she led them to a litter of seven fat little pups. Five were brown like their mom, and the other two were black and white. Glenda sat down beside them and picked each one up and caressed it.

"What do we do now?" Marcus asked.

Glenda handed him two pups. "We take them back to the car and the mom will follow."

That's what they did. Marcus carried four of them and Glenda carried three. The mom ran alongside with her tongue flopping and tail wagging.

When they got back to the Pit Stop, they found a stall for all of them together.

"Feels good, doesn't it?" Glenda asked.

Marcus nodded with a big smile. "It really does."

"Now we need to find them homes." Glenda batted her eyes quickly at Marcus.

"Oh no. I already have three from here, and I don't have room for those. If I bring another one home, my wife will leave me."

As they walked back toward the office, they could hear the phone ring.

A young volunteer stepped in and answered the phone. "Hello? The Pit Stop."

"Yes, I need to speak with Glenda Eagle, please." Dr. McNair's voice came through.

A girl stuck her head out the door. "Glenda—telephone."

Glenda Eagle walked Marcus to his car and thanked him again, not just for today, but for the dogfighting incident as well. She looked up at the volunteer. "Tell 'em I'm busy."

The teenage girl did just that.

"Tell her it's Dr. Stephen McNair."

"He says his name is Dr. Stephen McNair."

Glenda forgot to say good-bye to Marcus and turned and rushed to the phone. "Stephen, what's going on? Have you heard about the alien invasion? Is this what you meant when you told me the world was going to end?" There was a slight pause while she listened. "Okay, I'll stop talking so you can talk."

Several of the volunteers stopped what they were doing to watch Glenda, and even though she didn't say anything for a while, her eyes conveyed that whatever she was hearing was big. Finally, she got off the phone and looked at the ones gathered around.

"We have a lot of work to do." She pulled out the list of all the shelters, pounds, and humane societies in Southern California and dialed the first number. "Hello, this is Glenda Eagle with the Pit Stop. Do not, I repeat *do not*, put any pit bulls to sleep in the next week. The government will be sending a truck to pick them up. We need them to save the world."

After several more minutes of explaining the situation, she convinced the person on the other end of the line she wasn't pulling a prank. Glenda knew several of the larger shelters euthanized two hundred pit bulls a day, and she had the phone numbers of all of them, large and small. Plus, she knew of twelve other shelters like hers, and although none of them was quite as large as hers, together they cared for thousands of pits.

"What's going on?" one of her volunteers asked.

Glenda looked up and smiled. "They need as many pit bulls as they can get to stop the alien invasion." She walked out and looked down the long corridor of stalls housing most of the dogs and pointed. "Uncle Sam needs you."

The small group of volunteers all looked at each other for several seconds. Finally, the same one spoke again. "All right. Just tell us what we need to do."

Over the next few days, cattle and sheep trailers pulled by military trucks and driven by military personnel began showing up at all the places Glenda had provided the information for and had personally spoken to. After the trailers were loaded to the max, a two-man team would begin the roughly 2,700-mile drive to where the colonel and major awaited their new soldiers. The teams drove almost nonstop, taking turns to sleep.

Several trucks pulled up to the Pit Stop. Glenda directed the drivers where to park, and her volunteers started bringing the dogs to the trailers.

"Go get 'em, Emily," Glenda said as they loaded a red-and-white pit. "You be safe, Max," she said to a large brown pit. "Make us proud, Minnie," she said to another. "Take care, Buster. Be strong, Romeo. We love you, Clark Kent."

"Excuse me, ma'am," a private said. "This manifest says you have almost a thousand pit bulls. Is that right?"

"Goodbye, Barney." She looked at the private. "Yes, that's right. Why? We'll miss you, Ranger."

"I was just wondering, ma'am. Do you know all of them by

name?'

"Of course," Glenda snapped. "You got a problem with that?"

"No, ma'am, not at all." The private walked away and left Glenda to say farewell to all her pitties.

Soon her dogs were all loaded, and those trucks headed south like the others.

Back in Mexico, the command center received its first shipment of large plastic containers. Colonel Jamison rode with Darren and Francisco from one coast to the other explaining what was going on. The three pit bull lovers were enthusiastic. And for the first time since this war began, the soldiers had real hope.

After the large containers were spaced out all across the front line, the trucks with water and dog food began arriving. Just as the soldiers began to fill the containers, the colonel stopped them.

"Wait," the colonel said. "Let's relocate all the containers. Let's take them all up near the shield. Let's have the dogs set up there."

Everyone looked confused but followed the orders.

"Why up there, Colonel?" Darren asked.

The colonel smiled. "You'll see."

The containers were relocated right by the shield and were filled, one with water, the next with food, and so on until all were full. The huge fans also arrived and were positioned across the area to provide a breeze for the dogs.

The next day, Francisco rushed into the command center. "The dogs are coming."

Everyone except Sally went out to meet them. "I'm going to stay here and watch Angel," she said. "The thought of that many dogs all in one place scares me to death."

"Thank you," the colonel said and went outside with the others.

"Where do we unload them?" one of the drivers asked.

"All the way up there where the food and water is," said the colonel. "Just let them out."

The truck driver pulled up to the shield, made a large circle,

151

and backed the trailer up to within a hundred feet of the shield. Everyone except Sally was there when the first trailer doors were opened. The pit bulls just stood there not knowing what to expect. The driver came around and pulled out a sliding ramp and locked it into place. Still the dogs didn't budge.

Colonel Jamison walked up the ramp and started petting the dogs, who were all too eager to get some attention. "Come on, boys!" he yelled enthusiastically and ran down the ramp. Like a dam bursting, they all followed.

The dogs were happy to finally be out of the trailer and ran and jumped all over the place. All of them eventually found the water and food and helped themselves. Most of them still wanted attention and the soldiers were all too happy to oblige. Of course the colonel, Darren, and Francisco loved having so many pit bulls around.

As this truck pulled away slowly, another was making its circle and backed into place. These pit bulls could hardly wait for the ramp to be in place before hurrying off the trailer and into the open air.

Truck after truck unloaded thousands of happy, healthy pit bulls from California, then slowly drove away to keep from running over any of them. From here it was a short drive to several dozen shelters in Mexico.

The dogs were all shapes, sizes, and colors. Some had clipped ears, some had clipped tails, but all looked like great pit bulls.

"When does the shield lift?" the major asked the colonel over the sound of all the dogs.

"Should be tomorrow."

The major nodded. "I can't wait to see the look on their faces."

The colonel couldn't either.

Although the dogs wandered around out of curiosity, they all stuck close to the food and soldiers, who had moved their tents and sleeping bags up by the shield as well.

That evening in the command center, Colonel Jamison had everyone sit around the table. "I'm not sure if any of you are religious, but does anyone mind if I say a prayer for us tomorrow?"

Everyone shook their heads.

The colonel bowed his head and closed his eyes. "Heavenly Father, we turn to you in our moment of crisis. Please guide us tomorrow as we do what we think is right. Please watch over all the soldiers and all the wonderful pit bulls. In Jesus's name we pray. Amen."

Several others echoed the "amen." Francisco pulled a cross out from under his shirt, which was at the end of a gold chain around his neck, and kissed it. "Amen," he repeated.

"Let's get some rest tonight, my friends," the colonel said. "Tomorrow is sure to be an interesting day."

Everyone went to their respective sleeping quarters. Thomas walked Sally back to her tent, because she was still nervous about being around so many dogs. But they did make her think of Bully, the puppy Thomas had gotten her as a get-well-soon gift.

"Do you think it will work?" Sally asked.

Thomas nodded. "If you had seen what we saw when Angel tore into that alien, you'd be a believer too."

"I just want it to be over with no more killing," Sally said. "I'm going to have nightmares for the rest of my life. I hate these aliens. Why did they have to come here?"

Thomas put his arm around her. "Don't worry; it's going to work. I have all the faith in the world, and you know what a skeptical person I am. I don't usually believe in anything."

Sally laughed out loud. "How can you make me laugh at a time like this?"

Thomas smiled. "Just trying to keep the mood light. Just think, in a few days everything will be back to normal. You'll be swimming with friendly dolphins, Dr. McNair will be naming storms with human names, Darren will go back to SETI a hero, and I'll write another book that someone might actually read this time."

"You mean besides Darren?" Sally asked.

"Exactly. And when I ask you out for a date, you'll roll your eyes and tell me to 'dream on.'"

Sally smiled and put her hand on Thomas's hand, the one on

her shoulder. "Yes, that sounds about right."

The colonel's quarters were in the command center vehicle, and he and Angel turned in for the night. But slumber evaded the colonel for the better part of the night. There was just too much anticipation. Finally, in the wee hours of the morning, he drifted off to sleep. But it was not uneventful sleep.

"Hello, Daddy."

The colonel looked down at his daughter, Victoria. They were in the jungle again. But this time the colonel wasn't afraid. He knelt beside his daughter and gave her a kiss on the cheek. "You're so beautiful. You know that?"

She giggled. Then she looked into the forest. "Daddy, the monsters are coming. Aren't you scared?"

"No, sweetie. Not this time."

Angel came running up from nowhere.

"You remember Angel, don't you sweetie?"

"Yes," Victoria said and began patting Angel on the head.

The monsters came rushing through the jungle but stopped cold in their tracks. Angel barked and another dog that looked just like Angel appeared, then another and another. Soon there were thousands of her. They ran toward the monsters, who threw down their weapons and fled through the forest.

"I think you're going to be okay now, Daddy."

The colonel hugged his daughter tightly and stood up. "Me too, sweetie. You go on now and play. Daddy will see you soon."

Victoria giggled and ran away.

The colonel lay down in the jungle and drifted off to a peaceful sleep.

19

The colonel had the men get up at the break of dawn and move the food, water containers, and huge fans back behind the new dye line. The new spikes always measured off the exact same amount of area, so as the land became wider, the distance the aliens were moving became shorter and shorter. In the beginning, the spikes fell at least twenty miles north, but now it was barely eight miles. The Army Corps of Engineers was able to calculate the new area each time pretty accurately, so the dye lines could be marked well in advance.

"Be careful," the colonel ordered over the radio. "Watch where you step."

Now everyone understood why the colonel had the dogs stay up near the shield. The soldiers found it very difficult to maneuver themselves around all the gifts the dogs had left them on the ground.

"You wanted some land mines, Major," the colonel said to Major Strafford. "You've got plenty."

The major laughed and went to join his men.

The alarm sounded and the shield lifted. The alien troops came running out but quickly stopped. The colonel watched with his field glasses and began to laugh.

"What's happening?" Thomas asked.

"They hit the doggie gifts," the colonel said. "Some are shaking their feet trying to get the poop off; some are trying to sniff their feet. A couple slid down. It's hilarious."

The entire garrison of alien soldiers tried everything to get the sticky, smelly substance off their feet. Some grabbed leaves or sticks and began wiping, others slid their feet along the ground, and others shook their feet violently in an effort to rid them of the excrement. The dog poop did its job to slow the aliens down, but it was temporary. They soon regained their composure and kept coming.

The colonel gave the order and the soldiers advanced. Not knowing what was going on, most of the dogs followed. The colonel had ordered the jeeps to advance first for fear of running over some of the dogs, so everyone proceeded on foot after the jeeps had gotten way out in front.

Once the front line reached about halfway through the cleared area, the aliens appeared, running through the trees. Seeing the thousands of pit bulls, they stopped in their tracks and looked around at each other. One of them pulled up his weapon and fired.

That was the cue. The soldiers began rushing toward the enemy. Some of the dogs continued to follow. Other dogs apparently didn't know what was going on, or what was expected of them, and ran the other way. But most were just confused.

The aliens began firing at everything, but were having little luck. The pit bulls continued to scatter in all directions.

"They're not engaging," the colonel said, watching the battle again from the rear.

"Why not?" asked Francisco, who was sitting in the jeep with the colonel.

The colonel wasn't sure. He looked at Darren and Thomas, who stood beside their jeep.

"They don't know they're the enemy, Colonel," Darren said.

The colonel realized he was right. "Are you ready, son?" he asked Francisco.

"Yes, sir. What's the plan?"

The colonel smiled. "We're going right after one of them. You take out his weapon and we'll take him on mano a mano."

"Are you crazy, sir?" Thomas asked. "You will be no match for him hand to hand. He'll tear you to pieces."

"Exactly," the colonel said. "That's what riled up Angel. She had no problem knowing who the enemy was after that." The colonel sped away with Francisco clutching his rocket launcher.

"But that was your own dog," Darren yelled, but his words did not reach the speeding jeep, so he looked at Thomas. "It was his dog. I mean, that's why she attacked. Right?"

Thomas watched the jeep speed into the war zone and shrugged. "I don't know, Darren. I just don't know."

The colonel pointed to an alien and Francisco gave him a thumbs-up. As they neared, Francisco aimed and fired. It was a direct hit on the alien's weapon.

The alien tried firing it at the colonel and Francisco, but it wouldn't fire. Obviously angry, he threw the weapon aside and rushed toward them. This was common procedure. Whenever the aliens would fire their guns until the charge was gone, they fought with their bare hands, which were almost as deadly as their guns.

The colonel stopped the jeep. "Are you ready, son?"

"Nope."

The colonel laughed as both he and Francisco jumped out of the jeep. The creature advanced. The colonel took his sidearm and emptied the clip as the bullets ricocheted off the armor. The pair spread out as the alien neared them. He looked at Francisco first, then rushed the colonel. Francisco jumped on the alien's back and began stabbing him with his knife. The colonel rushed him from the front.

The large creature was not amused. He grabbed Francisco with one big hand and the colonel with the other as they both cried out for help. He tossed the colonel to the ground hard and rammed Francisco to the ground with his massive hand crushing him.

"Help!" Francisco cried out weakly.

And help arrived. A stout pit bull rushed the alien and launched into the air, clamping its teeth down on the creature's exposed underarm.

The alien soldier cried out in pain and released Francisco as he concentrated on his new adversary. He shook his arm wildly, trying to free himself of the canine, but the dog's jaws were closed tightly.

In desperation, the alien started punching the pit bull. After several punches, the dog had no choice but to release its grip.

But that was the key that set the chain reaction in motion. Several pit bulls nearby rushed the alien and began attacking. And they were smart. They rushed behind him and attacked him where there was no armor. The alien yelled out in agony.

The alien swung wildly at the dogs but to no avail. He tried charging, but the dogs quickly moved and continued to get behind him.

Soon other pits arrived and joined in on the attack. They launched into the air and bounced off the alien's chest and legs. Some concentrated on his exposed toes. Others clamped down on his calves and shook their heads violently.

The alien fell to his hands and knees and the dogs' attacks became even more brutal, tearing away at his face and neck. There were now over ten pit bulls attacking the one alien, and there was nothing he could do but curl into a ball and try to cover himself with his massive arms. He cried out again in pain as if begging for mercy. Other aliens nearby saw their comrade in arms struggling to survive, but were too afraid to come to his aid.

There was nothing left to do but tuck tail and run. The alien painfully got to his feet and tried to brush some of the dogs off of him so he could retreat. That too was futile as the dogs ran faster and were relentless in their attack. The alien went down again and again.

Across the entire battlefield, the dogs now knew who the enemy was. Thousands of them lunged for the aliens. Some of the aliens fired their weapons wildly, but could not hit their targets. Soon all the ammo was spent and the aliens were forced to confront their new attackers hand to hand, or hand to mouth to be more accurate. It was a decidedly one-sided battle.

Amazingly, the dogs began to form a strategy. As a dozen or so pit bulls would attack, many others would form a line behind the alien. If a dog were successfully pushed aside, another would jump right in and take its place. If the alien were somehow able to get free enough to make a run for it, he had a line of pits waiting to engage.

The aliens had no defense against the attacks. All they could eventually do was turn and try to run, and that made it much worse for them as it exposed their unprotected back sides. The cries rang out all over the battlefield, and it was a gruesome thing to be sure. These mighty warriors from outer space sounded like lambs in a slaughter. It was an eerie thing to hear.

Soldiers rushed to join the battle as alien after alien fell to the ground in an attempt to cover themselves from the dogs. Soldiers easily terminated them in this position.

With over half the alien forces out of commission and the rest still under heavy attack, the creatures made a beeline back toward their ship. Half of those would not even make it back to the tree line. Every alien was being swarmed by as many pit bulls as could find a place to sink their teeth. It truly looked like humans being swarmed by bees as the alien invaders swung wildly and screamed out in pain.

The rest managed to get into the trees, and the foliage and undergrowth hampered the dogs' maneuverability somewhat, giving the aliens a temporary reprieve to make a decent run for it. But they were in for a very unpleasant surprise. As they neared the old dye line, where the spikes currently were erected off each coast, the tops of the spikes were illuminated again. That only happened when they activated the shield.

And that's what had happened. As the fleeing aliens ran with all their might back toward the safety of their ship, they ran directly into the invisible shield, right where it had been this morning before lifting.

Some bounced backward hard as the momentum and weight of their bodies suddenly hit the transparent barrier. Several went down hard, only to jump up and rush forward again, beating their fists on the shield as if begging to be let in. Panic struck their faces as they realized their colleagues were protecting the ship from the new weapons. Fear struck their faces as they realized they were not going to be saved. Hatred struck their faces as they realized they were expendable. Some tried to climb the shield. Others turned and fought bravely. Nothing helped.

The colonel almost felt sorry for them. Almost. He gave the order for the soldiers to finish off all of them. The troops advanced to find the remaining alien forces sitting with their backs against the shield, trying to cover themselves from the ongoing attacks. The human soldiers moved the hordes of pit bulls away and terminated each alien without mercy.

The day was won.

Major Strafford came by in his jeep to pick up the colonel and Francisco, both still shaken from the fight. "Come on, let's end this."

The colonel smiled. The deep red marks were still visible around his neck. He looked around and saw Francisco still on the ground. He and the major rushed to him.

"Are you okay?" the colonel asked.

Francisco sat up slowly and clutched his throat. "I can hardly breathe. He almost crushed me."

"Thank goodness that pit bull came when he did," the colonel said.

Francisco nodded and looked around and saw the pit bull lying motionless on the ground. "No, no, no," he whispered and began crawling on the ground toward the dog. Tears began falling from his eyes.

"We need to go," the major said.

"You guys go ahead," Francisco said and kept crawling toward the pit bull.

The colonel nodded and he and the major drove away.

Francisco reached the dog and started running his hands though his fur. "You crazy dog." He lay across him gently and started kissing his head. He then sat up and lifted the dog's head and placed it in his lap. Tears continued streaming down Francisco's face as he ran his hands over the familiar white fur with black speckles and the brindled saddle shape over the dog's back. "I didn't even know you were here. You're going to be okay, Gentle Beast. You're going to be okay."

Thomas, Sally, and Darren had stood at the command center watching the battle unfold. They cheered as it became clear the plan had worked.

"Guys?" Sally said and tapped Thomas on the shoulder. "Guys, look."

The two men followed the direction of Sally's finger and saw what she saw; a man was walking toward them carrying a dog in his arms. As the figure got closer, they realized it was Francisco and rushed to his aid.

"Help us," Francisco said as they ran up to him. "Please help us."

Sally examined the dog in his arms and took charge. "Darren, put a blanket over the conference table. Thomas, go get a medic."

Francisco carried Gentle Beast into the command center and placed him on the makeshift gurney. As the medic arrived with her pack, she and Sally began working on Gentle Beast.

"His face looks pretty bad," Sally said.

Francisco smiled. "No, that's just his face."

Back in the field, the major and the colonel headed back to the camp. About halfway back, the colonel told Major Strafford to stop.

"What is it, sir?" the major asked.

"This is ours," the colonel said.

The major looked confused.

"This is ours," the colonel repeated. "We won this today. We don't move back anymore. Bring the command center here."

The major grinned. "Yes, sir." He got on the radio and passed along the order.

The command center, jeeps, and tents were moved to the south, and all the personnel set up camp. It marked the first time since the war began that new spikes would not fall and the shield would not be extended. It was also the first time the colonel allowed something else to happen. Unbeknownst to everyone, in the supply tents were cases of champagne and beer. He ordered them to be opened.

"Have a drink."

Francisco looked up and saw Sally holding a beer. He smiled and took it.

"I think he's going to be fine," Sally said, looking at Gentle Beast still on the table. He was bandaged so much only a few parts of his body were visible. A tube ran into his front leg from an IV. "You don't have to stay here. Why don't you come outside for a while?"

Francisco smiled. "I'm fine here. I don't want to leave him. Thanks for the beer."

Sally smiled and left.

"Come on, have a drink," Thomas said to Darren. "Celebrate. We just kicked some alien butt."

Darren looked up at Thomas and at the others standing outside the command center. "I don't know. I have a bad feeling."

Colonel Jamison, the only other person not celebrating, heard the conversation and walked over beside Darren. "What's on your mind, son?"

Darren shook his head. "Nothing has changed, sir. I know we won the battle today, and that's great, but the aliens are still here. I half expected them to fly back to their mother ship and for that ship to leave the orbit around Earth. But the aliens are still here and the mother ship is still out there. According to these current reports from NASA, nothing has changed."

"So you're saying they haven't given up?" the colonel asked.

Darren nodded. "That's what I'm afraid of."

"You think they'll be back tomorrow with more forces?" Thomas asked.

"Maybe," Darren said. "Maybe they'll be back tomorrow with something worse. I mean, we're talking about a civilization that has conquered space travel, among other technological achievements. What if they come back tomorrow with robots or something?"

Thomas searched the colonel's face for any expression. There was none.

"Major?"

The major walked over. "Yes, sir, colonel?"

"No more celebrating tonight," the colonel said. "Spread the word for everyone to be ready to fight tomorrow."

"Yes, sir." The major quickly left to deliver the orders.

"Okay, you guys are ruining my buzz," Thomas said. He walked over and stood beside Sally. "Cheers, honey bunny."

Sally smiled and bumped her champagne glass to Thomas's beer can.

After everyone else had turned in for the night, the colonel stayed up late with Darren as they considered every possible scenario. "I guess we won't really know until tomorrow," the colonel concluded before both he and Darren called it a night.

20

The colonel was up bright and early the next morning, walking through the ocean of pit bulls, taking time to pet each one in arm's reach. The food and water containers were still mostly full, and the colonel laughed to himself at all the fresh piles of doggie poop spread out all over the ground. He walked carefully as if he were stepping through a minefield.

As the others rose for the day and the soldiers began preparing themselves for whatever lay ahead, the colonel knelt down in the middle of all the dogs around him to say another prayer.

When the time neared that the shield would normally rise, he positioned himself on top of the command center for a better view. Using his field glasses, he watched for any sign of movement behind the shield. Finally he saw it, and it sent chills down his spine.

"You're not going to believe this!" he yelled down at the others.

Everyone looked up. "Oh no," Sally said. "What is it?"

The colonel continued to survey the enemy for several more seconds before lowering the field glasses and looking toward the ground where the others eagerly awaited the new information. He took a deep breath and said, "They have dogs."

Darren gasped. Of all the scenarios they had imagined, this was not one of them. He looked out at all the pit bulls, then back to the colonel. "Big dogs?"

The colonel nodded. "Humongous."

Word quickly spread down the front line, and the soldiers' demeanor began to affect the dogs. They could sense something was wrong but weren't sure what.

The colonel looked again and could see hundreds of giant dogs, and there was no telling how many were beyond his view. They were four times the size of the larger pit bulls, and like the aliens, they were very muscular with oversized heads. They were on long, thick leashes and were digging in their front paws, raring to go. But the big difference was the teeth. Whereas the colonel had never noticed the teeth of the aliens, the canines on these canines were extremely large.

The alarm sounded and the shield lifted as the aliens advanced with their dogs leading the way.

"What do we do, Colonel?" Francisco asked.

The colonel climbed down the ladder on the rear of the command vehicle. "Same as yesterday," he said. "Let's kick some butt."

The soldiers nearby began to cheer and the attitude swept down the front lines. The dogs reflected the excitement and followed the jeeps and soldiers southward to meet the enemy. This time the pit bulls had no trouble knowing who the enemy was.

As the aliens cleared the tree line, they released their dogs. The massive hounds sprang forward. They resembled charging rhinos. The ground shook as their huge paws impacted the ground beneath them.

The pit bulls were undaunted and charged ahead at full speed. For stocky, muscular dogs, some of the pits were amazingly fast.

The colonel watched as the two canine species neared each other. It reminded him of when he was a kid and played marbles. You had a few strikers, the larger marbles, and then many of the smaller ones.

The pits and alien dogs met in the middle of the clearing, and that's where the progress of the invaders stopped cold. The large alien dogs were powerful and mean to the core, but they were also bulky and slower than the Earth dogs. The pit bulls rushed them in numbers and attacked their vulnerable underbellies, legs, and paws. The large alien dogs lunged time and again toward a pit bull but came up empty. Yelps could be heard across the battlefield each time the powerful jaws of the pit bulls made contact.

Just like before, the pit bulls formed a strategy. But this time they formed close circles around the larger dogs and charged at will from any and all directions. The alien dogs had absolutely no defense against the onslaught of sharp teeth and the incredible strength of the jaw muscles of the pits.

The alien soldiers fired their weapons from the safety of the tree line, but hit empty ground, or sometimes their own dogs. They fired at will and soon their guns were out of power and useless.

The sun was barely halfway up the eastern sky when it became clear to everyone that this battle, like the one yesterday, was going to be decidedly one-sided. The large alien dogs fought bravely, but were simply outmatched in every way.

Within a couple of hours, the big alien dogs tucked tail and headed for the safety of their ship. When the soldier aliens saw them running back toward them, they panicked as well and turned to run back too.

Pit bulls followed them into the dense forest and pursued. And, like the day before, the aliens on the ship were taking no chances and the soldier aliens and giant dogs ran headfirst into the shield, which had been raised again without them knowing it.

And like the day before, they were easy pickings as the human troops quickly disposed of all the aliens and their pets trapped on this side of the shield.

When it was over, humans and pit bulls alike jumped up and down in celebration.

"We've got 'em beat, Colonel," Francisco said.

The colonel nodded. "Yes, we do, son. Yes, we do."

The colonel and Francisco drove back to the command center where most of the advisory group was likewise jumping up and down in celebration. The colonel got out of the jeep and hugged them individually as they all hugged one another. Everyone except Darren again.

The colonel noticed Darren's look of depression. "You're kidding me. They're still not leaving."

Darren shook his head as everyone else noticed something was wrong.

"What's going on?" Dr. McNair asked.

"The aliens are still here," Colonel Jamison said.

Everyone stopped celebrating.

Major Strafford rode up in his jeep, ready to celebrate too before seeing everyone's expression. "I take it they haven't left yet," he said as he got out of his vehicle.

The colonel nodded. He wondered how the aliens could be beaten so badly the last two days and still be ready for more. He looked out over the sea of pit bulls and had an idea. "Dr. Mitchell?"

"Yes, sir?" Darren walked over to the colonel.

The colonel considered how to phrase his thoughts. "You told us once that you guys have a language based on math that any intelligent creature can understand, right?"

"Yes, that's correct, Colonel."

Everyone walked a little closer to find out what the colonel was getting at.

"Okay," the colonel said. "Can you make it say anything you want?"

"I can't," Darren said. "But the people who developed it can make it say anything regarding a mathematical sequencing, I suppose."

"Great." The colonel walked a little closer to him. "Get them to make it say we have one million more pit bulls coming."

Darren's eyes were open wide. "Uh, Colonel, I'm not sure—"

"That is not a suggestion, Dr. Mitchell. Make it happen." The colonel turned his attention to Major Strafford. "Where are all the trucks and drivers that brought the pit bulls?"

"About twenty miles north, I think."

Darren stopped as he was about to enter the command center and turned back. "Colonel, one question. Do we really have a million more pit bulls coming?"

The colonel smiled. "No, son, it's called a bluff and we're going to play it without flinching."

The major laughed. "What's the plan?"

"Just tell the drivers to stand by. If we can get this message to say what we want it to say, we'll tell them what to do."

Everyone walked into the command center. Darren was already on the SATCOM speaking to his boss, Dr. De Luca.

"I know how it sounds," Darren said. "But we need this as soon as possible, like in an hour."

Everyone sat around waiting. Two hours later, Dr. De Luca called back. "We have it!" he almost yelled into the radio. "I'm sending it to you now. Be ready to record."

The mathematical message played as Darren recorded it. He then rigged the speakers on several jeeps again to play the message as loudly as possible.

"Come on, Francisco," the colonel said. "You and I will take one of the jeeps."

As the colonel got into the jeep, he nodded to the major. The major got on the radio and contacted the drivers. "Okay, men, bring all the trucks back and circle around and back them in just like you have a full load of pit bulls to unload."

"Major?" Darren said.

"Yes?"

"I think the enemy might have infrared capabilities."

The major shook his head. "Oh crap." He looked around at several soldiers standing nearby and smiled. "Okay, men, get everyone and meet the trucks and get into the trailers and everyone sit down."

The soldiers laughed and ran to get the others.

Colonel Jamison and Francisco reached the shield. He had the other jeeps spread out wide and all three began playing the recorded message, the huge speakers vibrating as they blared the recording.

Back at the command center, the trucks and trailers came rolling up loaded with soldiers and began backing up as if they were going to unload.

It worked. Suddenly the shield lifted. All of the spikes magically pulled out of the sandy bottom of the beaches and launched into the air. They sped upward and got smaller and smaller in perspective. A loud noise was heard and the wind hit the colonel's jeep with a force.

"Look," Darren yelled and pointed to the horizon.

Everyone turned to follow the direction of his finger.

"Oh my," Sally said.

The huge ship was leaving, and in a hurry. It didn't even bother to go to stealth mode. It was getting out of here as fast as possible. The gang watched it until it disappeared into the sky, and everybody cheered again.

The colonel breathed a sigh of relief. He drove back to the command center where everyone, including Darren, was jumping up and down.

"We did it, Colonel," Francisco said.

The colonel nodded and they joined the celebration of happy soldiers, joyful advisors, and ecstatic pit bulls.

"What now, Colonel?" Sally asked.

"We'll wait to hear from Washington, but I think it's over. I guess we can all go home," the colonel said.

"I want to stay and have a look at the alien constructions," Darren said.

"Me too," everyone else agreed.

"Makes sense to me," the colonel said with a smile. "But right now, I think I'm going to bed to see how long I can sleep." And after giving the news of the victory to General Nickerson, he did just that.

The next day, the Army Corps of Engineers showed up to inspect the buildings.

"They're magnificent, aren't they?" one of the engineers said to Darren.

"They really are," Darren agreed. "The roofs are some sort of solar panel, which not only converts the slightest sun rays to electricity, but also stores it so that the buildings have power overnight. It's incredible."

"I don't know what we will do with all of these," another engineer said.

Darren looked out over the terrain at all the pit bulls running and playing among themselves. "I think I know what we can do with a lot of these buildings," he said. "We need a temporary shelter for a whole lot of heroes."

The engineer smiled. "I think that can be arranged. We'll get cots, blankets, and plenty of food and water. I have a feeling that they'll be welcome here as long as it takes."

"Make sure to set up bathing and grooming areas and provide plenty of treats," Darren added.

Thomas, who had walked up during the conversation, tapped Darren on the shoulder. When Darren turned around, he raised his eyebrows.

Darren smiled. "Oh, and plenty of chew toys."

21

"Looks like love at first sight."

"You're right, Colonel," Darren said as he also looked at Roscoe and Angel, who had crawled up into a chair together and fallen asleep. He then turned to his former assistant, Rebecca, and kissed her on the lips. He looked deep into her beautiful brown eyes. "You're absolutely right, Colonel."

Rebecca smiled and kissed him back.

"How did you guys meet?" Belinda, the colonel's wife, asked.

"We both work for SETI," Darren explained.

Rebecca nodded. "That's right. He was my boss."

"Oh," Belinda said. "I see."

"Having fun, Stephen?" the colonel asked.

Dr. McNair was sitting on the hardwood flooring with a margarita in one hand. Glenda Eagle sat between his legs and was leaned back against his chest. She had a bottle of beer in her hand.

"Yes, sir, Colonel," Dr. McNair said. "Those were your orders, wasn't it?"

"Affirmative."

Everyone laughed.

"How about you, Ms. Escamilla?" asked Dr. McNair. "Are you and Maria enjoying yourself?"

"Very much so," Francisco's mom said. "I wasn't sure I would feel comfortable on the water, but it is really nice."

"Well, it helps that we're on a brand-new sixty-foot yacht," Darren said.

"I love it," said Maria, Francisco's little sister. "I hope Francisco catches some fish."

They all looked out on the huge back deck, where Francisco was the only person closely watching a fishing pole mounted into a holder on the back railing. Gentle Beast lay beside him, resting his huge head on Francisco's foot. These two were inseparable. Gentle Beast didn't like for Francisco to be more than six inches from him at all times. He was free of bandages but still walked with a limp and probably would the rest of his life. But he was very happy.

"You should be proud of him, Ms. Escamilla," the colonel said. "He is truly a hero."

Everyone nodded in agreement as Thomas came up the stairs from the lower deck. "Hero?" Thomas asked. "Is someone talking about me again?"

They all laughed.

"Hey, man, put a shirt on," the colonel said jokingly. "My wife hasn't seen a body like that since I was younger."

"Ha!" Belinda scoffed. "I've never seen a body like that."

This brought about more laughter. There was a great atmosphere aboard the boat. Emmanuel came down the stairs from the upper deck.

"Hey, little man," Dr. McNair said. "How are you doing?"

Emmanuel smiled. "Great, doc. This is awesome." He walked over to Maria. "Want me to show you the whole boat?"

Maria's eyes lit up. "Sure."

"Just a minute there, you little punk." Francisco had walked to the back entrance of the cabin, Gentle Beast right by his side. "That's my little sister."

Everyone laughed again as Emmanuel held his hands up in surrender. "I was just being friendly."

"Well, come on back here and show me how to catch some fish, Mr. Friendly."

As Francisco and Emmanuel reached the back of the boat, bubbles hit the surface, followed by the scuba diver. She removed her mouthpiece and climbed up the ladder.

Thomas met her at the back of the boat with a large beach towel. "Here you go, honey." After Sally took off the tank, he wrapped the towel around her and pulled her close. "How was it down there?"

"Beautiful," Sally said. "Why don't you come down with me next time?"

"Not a chance."

She laughed as their lips met in a long embrace.

"Hey, get a room you two," the colonel said.

"Can you teach me how to scuba dive?" Francisco asked.

"I would be happy to."

"I think you're crazy," Dr. McNair stated. "Do you not remember what happened the last time you went diving in this area?"

"I do remember," Sally said. "But Darren said the aliens are gone and the signal has disappeared. Right, Darren?"

Darren heard his name and stopped kissing Rebecca. "Hmm? What? Oh yeah, they're long gone. No trace of them."

"Do you think they'll return?" Glenda asked.

Darren patted Roscoe and Angel on their heads. "Nope. Not as long as we have our guardians." He leaned back over and kissed Rebecca again.

Thomas, Sally, Francisco, and Emmanuel all walked into the large cabin and found a seat. There was plenty of room for all of them.

Erique came down the stairs. "Hey, guys," he said.

"Hey, Erique," Sally said. "How do you like your new boat so far?"

"Are you kidding?" he joked. "Besides my family, this is the most beautiful thing I have ever seen. I cannot believe the United Stated government would buy it for me."

"Yes, who would have thought that the government would ever do anything right," Glenda said. "But they have really begun to take the overpopulation problem of pit bulls seriously. They've passed an emergency measure that no pits are to be euthanized, and they're drafting a bill to restrict unauthorized breeding."

"They had better," the colonel said. "Pit bulls saved the entire planet."

"That's true," Dr. McNair agreed. "I guess pits are not just America's dog anymore. They belong to the world."

"At least we have plenty of shelter space now," Glenda said, "thanks to the aliens."

"What do you mean?" Belinda asked.

"All the buildings, honey," the colonel said.

"That's right," Glenda said. "Since we now have all this cleared land and the pit bulls were already there, the US government worked with the other countries to use the buildings for shelters. We're getting thousands of applications every day from people all over the world wanting to adopt one of the pit bulls that saved the planet. It's all run by Francisco's friend Ms. Rhonda."

"She's great," Ms. Escamilla said. "They are in good hands."

Francisco nodded.

"Those buildings are extraordinary too," Darren said. "The aliens really were advanced in architecture as well. Not only can the building be erected with limited tools in a very short time, the entire roof is one giant solar conductor strong enough to provide power to the building even on stormy days. As soon as the building is set up, it already has electricity. It's ingenious."

"Well," Erique said, looking at his watch, "it's almost time."

He turned and walked back up the stairs. Everyone got up and followed. Once on the upper deck, Erique went on up to the captain's station while everyone else found a place along the railing of the top deck and looked out over the water.

In the distance, they could see two US battleships. Beyond that, although it was just open water, Sally, Thomas, Dr. McNair, and Erique knew the area well. It's where the aliens' wall had been constructed underwater.

The colonel pointed to the area and moved his finger slowly southward. "They tell me there are twenty-four nuclear subs under us right now awaiting launch orders."

"We're about to set the world back on path," Dr. McNair said.

"Amen," Thomas said.

"Amen indeed," the colonel echoed.

Several seconds passed as everyone stared toward the area past the battleships. Then it happened. A large blast of water shot several hundred feet into the sky, followed by another to the south, and another, until the blasts could no longer be seen. The sound of each torpedo slamming into the rock wall still carried well across the water, however, and everyone stayed until all ninety-six were heard, four from each submarine.

"Here's to cooler days," Dr. McNair said and raised his glass.

Everyone joined in on the toast, including Angel, Roscoe, and Gentle Beast, who barked their agreement.

***

Meanwhile, in a huge spacecraft swiftly leaving the Milky Way, the military leader of the alien forces was hearing it from the alien king, in their own language of course.

"You got beat by a bunch of primitive little people!" the king shouted as he walked around the great chamber. His robes flowed behind him and a crystal crown shone on his head. All of the royal subjects were there, as well as all the different commanders and leaders. "All of our time and resources wasted. I should have you terminated for incompetence."

The military leader stood with his head fixed, his eyes looking straight ahead but not focusing on anything. He didn't say a word, only taking his punishment in stride.

"What do we do now?" the king asked.

No one said anything.

He looked at his scientific leader. "Answer me!" he yelled. "What do we do next?"

The scientific leader began to shake. "Well, Your Majesty, there's a small planet in the Andromeda galaxy inhabited by a small, peaceful race of people whose technology is not yet far advanced. We should be able to colonize that planet rather easily."

"That's what you said about Earth," the king snapped. "What makes you think we can take over that planet so easily?"

The scientific leader swallowed hard. "Well, Your Majesty, for one thing, they have no pit bulls."

Pit Bulls vs. Aliens